UNKNOWN DESTINY

A Fantasy Novel

Johnnie West

Van Rye
PUBLISHING

Cover design by Vila Design

Published by Van Rye Publishing, LLC
Ann Arbor, MI
www.vanryepublishing.com

ISBN: 978-1-957906-08-9 (paperback)
ISBN: 978-1-957906-09-6 (ebook)
Library of Congress Control Number: 2022951793

Contents

Contents

Chapter 1

Stormy Night

JARED WAS AWOKEN by rain and wind one dark and stormy night. He heard thunder getting closer. He had hated lightning and thunder since he was a little boy. Lightning brought back memories of when he was a young boy camping in the mountains with his dad. There had been a freak rainstorm with lightning so close that they could feel the electricity in the air and thunder that felt like it was right on top of them. Since then, lightning and thunder frightened Jared so much that he would have panic attacks.

Now almost eighteen years old, Jared was thin and tall, standing approximately six feet with a wiry build. His brown hair had a natural curl that he hated, but all the girls seemed jealous of it. His blue eyes were like the color of the Caribbean Sea, and when he smiled, he had dimples that everyone loved. He was popular with all the girls.

Jared was lying in bed, thinking about his life. He lived at home with his parents and two younger sisters who were twins. If Jared had to choose one, the youngest of the twins would be his favorite one. Jared and his dad, the only males in the family, stuck together like glue.

The floor of Jared's twelve-foot by twelve-foot room was cluttered with both clean and dirty clothes like most teenage boys' rooms were. He had a closet, but he was a little claustrophobic, so he didn't put clothes in the closet. Instead, he mostly used the closet for storing things he didn't use much.

The storm was getting closer. Jared counted the seconds between the lightning and the crackling of the thunder. He was barely getting up to five seconds between the two. His heartbeat increased with every lightning strike. He knew the storm was almost right on top of the house. Jared's family lived in the suburbs in Colorado, close to a mountain range. The storms there could get bad. It was 11 p.m., and this was a normal summer storm. But to Jared, the storms there seemed to happen frequently—*too* frequently. And his phobia about them didn't make the severe storms any easier for him to handle.

Jared's house was quiet except for the sounds of the storm. Then, lightning hit somewhere nearby, and the flash brightened Jared's bedroom. He jumped and ran out of his room. He headed to the kitchen to get a drink of water. The kitchen was just down the hall from Jared's bedroom and to the left. Being in the roomier kitchen made Jared feel better because it didn't feel as confining as his bedroom. He flipped on the light so that he didn't run into anything with his bare feet.

There was another strike and then a crashing sound, one second apart. Jared dropped his water but managed to grab it before it hit the floor. Then, the power went out, and he was standing in the dark kitchen, unable to see until his eyes got accustomed to the dark again. As he was standing there, feeling the cold floor on his feet, Jared could hear the wind causing the windows to bow. The wind was so strong that he thought the glass was going to break. The storm was increasing in strength. It was right on top of the house now.

Lightning, then thunder, then lightning again. Jared thought it would never end. Then, he saw an *extremely* bright flash, but this one was green. Jared had never seen green lightning before. The flash was so bright that he could have sworn it was right in the backyard. But the sound that should have accompanied the lightning was not a crackling snap, just a very low thud that Jared could feel in his chest.

Jared ran to the window. The window felt cold and damp to the touch. He peered out into the backyard and noticed that the glowing green light had not dissipated like regular lightning does. The glow lit up the entire backyard. Jared knew something was different about the green glow; he just didn't know what. Everyone in the house was still asleep. Jared was the only one who hated the summer storms enough to be awake and cowering. As he leaned against the glass, which was flexing from the wind, he could see a green glowing object in the backyard that was letting off steam as the rain hit it.

Jared wanted badly to go outside and see what the object was, but the storm was right over the house now, and he didn't want to be stuck outside in it. But he also didn't want to wait until morning to investigate the object, for fear that someone else might find it before him. Jared's backyard was part of a community backyard, so many homes surrounded his yard. Someone else could easily find the object before he did.

After thinking for a few minutes, Jared returned to his room to grab a raincoat and shoes. As soon as he had them on, he went back to the kitchen and looked out the window again at the object. He was going to brave the storm. He knew that with all the noise from the wind, rain, and thunder, no one in his family would hear him go outside. The back door opened easily, even with the wind pushing against it. Jared just needed to make sure the door did not slam against the wall.

With the door open and the wind now blowing into the house, the rain was soaking the kitchen floor. So, Jared quickly jumped out into the rain and shut the door behind him. Then, he looked over at the glowing object. Steam was still coming off the object, so Jared figured it must have been hot when it landed on the ground. The glow was not as strong as it had been when Jared first observed the object, shortly after it hit the ground. But the object was still dazzling as it shone through the darkness of the night.

The rain was pelting Jared's body. Even with a raincoat on, he could feel rain soaking him. The water was hitting his head, wetting his brown hair and bringing out the curls he hated so much, then rolling down his neck and into his raincoat. Jared was so mesmerized by the glow that he didn't even startle with the continued lightning strikes and crashing thunder. He just stood in the rain, admiring the beautiful green glow. It was hypnotizing. Then, a crack of lightning startled him and finally snapped him out of his trance.

Jared walked closer to the object but still couldn't tell what it was. He could only tell that it was oval-shaped and extremely smooth. The closer Jared got to the object, the more he could

4

feel the heat radiating from it. He was amazed that it was still hot since the rain had been soaking it for five minutes. He again became hypnotized by the object and unaware that his raincoat had come open and that he was now dripping wet. The object seemed to call to him. Jared couldn't actually hear anything but could feel a connection to the pulsating glow, and he found that his breathing matched the pulsating pattern of the mysterious object. As he would breathe in, the glow would intensify. The opposite happened when he exhaled.

It felt to Jared like he had been standing in the rain for at least an hour, but he had only been outside for ten minutes. As he got closer to the object, he could tell that its heat was finally being tamped down by the rain. Jared kneeled on the wet grass and put his hands out to feel the warmth of the glow. It felt calming and relaxing. The lightning and thunder did not seem to bother Jared anymore. The green object was doing something to him, but what? With the object hypnotizing him with its glowing properties and warmth, Jared felt more relaxed than he ever had in a lightning storm.

Though Jared had an urge to touch the object, he was cautious. It was a mysterious item that he had never seen the likes of before. But as the feeling intensified, he knew he had to touch it. Jared's hands seemed to move on their own, hovering over the object and then falling right onto it before he even realized what he was doing. As soon as contact was made, Jared felt a surge of energy that was almost overwhelming to his senses. The feeling was addicting, and he could not bring himself to raise his hands off the smooth green object. Jared was so enthralled with the object that he didn't even notice that

5

the wind had blown his raincoat open. He was now completely soaked.

The longer Jared's hands were on the object, the more he sensed he was not alone. Then, out of the corner of his eyes, he saw someone walking by. He shifted his gaze from the green glow to his left side. No one was there. But Jared knew he had seen someone or . . . some*thing*. He grabbed the object and held it in his arms. He didn't even notice the large hole the object had left in the grass because he was too busy admiring the object's beauty up close and enjoying the warmth it was radiating. There were strange designs on the sides, like swirls and lines traveling through them. The object felt like a rock that had been smoothed and put through a rock tumbler and then cut into an oval-shaped egg. It was about eleven inches long and six inches tall.

Jared again saw movement off to his side. He glanced in the direction of the movement, but nothing was there. He was still alone. Jared finally became fully aware of his surroundings again. The storm was strong, and Jared realized that the rain had soaked every inch of him. Lightning flashed with a crackling sound of electricity. He had never heard it like that before. He could hear the lightning as it was moving through the sky, and he no longer felt scared of it. His fear of lightning and thunder was gone.

After snapping back into reality, Jared exclaimed out loud, "I need to get out of the rain!" He stood up and cradled the oval stone inside his coat, carrying it like a newborn baby, protecting it. He turned, and as he walked toward the back door of his home in his wet sloshing shoes, he saw movement again. It was not threatening movement. To Jared, it felt more like he was seeing another reality on top of his own reality, all at the same time. Then, the movement would disappear as fast as it had shown up.

Jared made it to the door and opened it, being careful not to let it slam into the wall. Then, he shut it behind him. The power was still out, but Jared had the glow of the stone to light the way to his room. He walked through the kitchen, but the squeaking and sloshing of his shoes were too noisy, so he slid them off and carried them to his room. Having wet feet on the kitchen's tile floor made it tricky to walk across without slipping and falling.

It was ten minutes to midnight. Fifty minutes had gone by since Jared left his room, but to him, it felt like he had been outside for only a few minutes. Where had the time gone? Back in his room, Jared placed the glowing egg on his dresser, and then he put on some dry clothes and sat down on his bed. He now found the sound of thunder exhilarating as the sound moved through his body. These feelings Jared was experiencing were new to him. He was no longer tired. Even though it was the middle of the night, he was wide awake. All he wanted to do was to hold the rock and feel it close to him. It still felt like it was calling to him.

Jared got off his bed and walked over to the amazing, glowing oval. He picked it up and held it. As soon as he picked it up, he saw movement again out of the corner of his eyes. Jared shifted his glance to the side of his room. This time, he saw a strange new world. He saw magical creatures and people doing things that looked like magic to him, and the people were doing it without moving. They were talking but making no sounds, and they were moving things with their minds. The people and creatures were holding rocks that were changing color and size.

The new world Jared could see suddenly disappeared when he set the green object down. He was alone in his room again. The day before, he had tripped and cut his arm on a fence. But when he looked down at his arm, he noticed that the cut was gone. There was no sign of it ever being there.

The wonderment of the stone was streaming through Jared's head. Had the egg-shaped object healed him? Was it giving him the ability to see another world that sat right on top of his own world? He was unsure. He was quite sure the egg was the center of everything that was happening in his room, but where did it come from? The storm was passing. The rain was letting up, and so was the wind. Jared could still hear thunder, but it was off in the distance.

Jared placed the stone back on his dresser and got into bed. As he did, he looked over at his clock, which reflected that an hour had gone by since he had reentered his room. Jared thought, *That can't be right. I just walked into my room ten minutes ago!* But he shook it off and closed his eyes to go to sleep. Even though he was not exhausted like he was when the storm woke him up, it was late. He and his dad had plans to go fishing the next day.

After about an hour of trying to get to sleep, Jared finally found himself in dreamland. But it was not like any dream he had ever had. He dreamed of a world that had fairies and magical beings. He could see all these new things, but he could not interact with any of them. And though he could see them, they could not see him.

Jared slept through the night and woke early in the morning. The first thing he saw when he woke up was the green rock. He knew he had to hide it somewhere in his room so that his sisters and parents couldn't find it until he wanted it to be known to them. He put it in his closet and was surprised to discover that he was not even nervous about stepping inside. Then, he left the room.

As Jared entered the kitchen, he noticed that his mom and dad were looking out the back door. They were wondering why the kitchen floor was wet and how a big hole had been made in their backyard. When Jared walked over to the back door and looked for himself, he was shocked that the hole was so big. He didn't remember the hole being that big when he viewed it at night.

Two neighbors were out looking at the hole as well, so Jared's dad, Dave, went out to discuss the situation with them. The neighbors told Dave that they remembered seeing a shadow of someone approximately six feet tall out in the yard late in the night, around midnight, but that they had been unable to make out the person's features. That was all they could recall. When Dave went back into the house, he saw Jared and asked him if he knew anything about the hole in the yard.

"All I remember is the big storm we had last night," Jared lied.

Dave knew about Jared's fear of lightning and thunder, so he said, "With the storm last night, I know you wouldn't have gone out there."

While Jared's mother, Heather, was cleaning up the wet floor, she asked, "Can anyone tell me how the floor got so wet during the night?" But no one answered her. Jared kept his head down and did not make eye contact with his mother. She could always tell if someone was not being truthful with her, so Jared didn't want to lie to her.

Dave walked over to Jared, put his arm over his son's shoulders, and said, "It's Saturday. Should we go fishing?"

Jared's mother cut in, saying, "The yard needs to be fixed, and the grass needs to be mowed before you two do anything else today."

"We'll get it done this morning," Dave reassured her. "And then we can go do something." As he looked at Jared and smiled, he told him to go get dressed.

Dave was an average-sized man. He had a bit of a gut and was not as tall as Jared. He was going bald on top, so he liked to wear baseball caps. Dave kept his hair and mustache short, but he was self-conscious about the thinning on top. He would always tell Jared, "Enjoy your hair while you have it because this is your future someday." Jared would just laugh.

Jared returned to his room and wondered if the night's events were just a dream and the rock he found was just a green rock. He pulled the rock out from his closet and held it with both hands. As he did, he looked around, but there was nothing like what he had seen the night before. *Maybe it really was all a dream*, he thought. But no, Jared was sure that what he remembered seeing and feeling during the night really happened. After shrugging his shoulders, Jared put the rock back in his closet and got dressed. Despite his newfound confidence around the closet, he was still not thrilled about leaning into it to put the rock on the floor.

Once Jared was dressed, he went into the kitchen and ate the breakfast his mom had put out on the table. It was bacon and eggs with toast and honey and some orange juice to rinse it all down. As Jared was eating, his twin sisters came into the room.

Anna, the older twin by three minutes, liked to tease Jared. She sat across from him and said, "I heard you up late last night. What were you doing?" She was trying to get Jared in trouble. She was *always* trying to do that.

Jared tried to ignore Anna, but she kept pushing him until his mom told her, "Stop bothering your brother!"

The two sisters were sixteen, and the younger one was not like Anna at all. She just sat and quietly ate her breakfast, leaving Jared alone. Her name was Stephany, and she loved to follow Jared around. She found him fascinating to be around. And Jared felt protective of her.

The twins were each about five feet five inches tall, so they were quite a bit shorter than Jared. They were both thin with blonde, wavy, flowing hair and blue eyes. They were the popular girls at school, and Anna always reminded Jared that she had more friends than him. But Jared ignored her as much as he could.

"Are you about done eating, Jared?" his mother asked as she reached to take his almost-empty plate. "If you are, your dad is outside waiting for you."

Jared took one last bite and a swallow of orange juice and then headed outside to the backyard. Stephany chased right after him, but Jared didn't mind. He was used to her being around him.

Dave handed Jared a shovel and told him to smooth out the hole in the grass. The hole was about two feet deep and three feet wide, so it was going to take a little work to fill in. As Jared began working on the hole, Dave pushed a wheelbarrow full of dirt over to it. He had already been to the garden store and picked up the dirt to fill the hole in with. Dave approached Jared and asked, "Are you sure you know nothing about this hole in the grass?"

Jared hesitated for a moment, then shrugged. "I don't know how the hole got in the grass."

"But the neighbors swear they saw you out here around midnight. What is the truth?"

"I did not make the hole, Dad."

Dave decided not to push the issue, so he left it alone.

It was going to be a beautiful, sunny day, and it was already getting hot. Jared was glad they started working early in the day when it was cooler. It only took about half an hour to fill in the hole and repatch the grass. As soon as that was done, Jared's father told him to mow the lawn before the day got any hotter.

Jared pulled the lawn mower out from the garage and mowed the lawn while Stephany sat on the porch and watched him work. The girls rarely had to do any yard work. Dave always said, "It is the man's job to do yard work." Jared thought that comment was unfair, but he just did what he was told.

Jared was getting sweaty from working in the sun, but he

was almost done with the yard work, and then he could go inside and cool off. As soon as he finished, he put the mower away and headed back into the house, then went to his room to change his clothes. He went into his closet, and as he grabbed the green rock to move it out of the way, he felt the surge of electricity all over again. This time, it startled him, so he quickly dropped the rock and yelled, "Ouch!" He knew he was not imagining it this time!

Heather heard Jared yell and came knocking at his door, asking him if everything was alright.

"Yeah, Mom. I just dropped something on my foot, and it hurt," Jared replied.

"Okay, just be careful, honey."

Heather looked like a beauty queen. Like Jared, she was around six feet tall. She had long blonde hair and an athletic build, and she wore little makeup. Her blue eyes were so ocean blue that they looked like they were glowing. It was obvious where the three kids got their eye color from. Jared took after his mom with his looks and height, and the girls took after their dad with their height.

From watching Jared mow the lawn, Stephany could tell that something had changed in him. She was determined to find out what. So, she decided to follow him around all day until she knew his secret.

When Jared was done changing his clothes, he needed to hide the egg, but he was afraid to touch it again. So, he kicked it to the bottom of his closet until it was in the back corner again. He then came out of his room and ran directly into Stephany, who said, "I know you have a secret, Jared."

13

"Mind your own business, Stephany!" Jared retorted. Then, he walked away. Jared usually wasn't cross with Stephany, but he wanted to keep the rock that he found to himself.

Stephany could now *really* tell that Jared had changed. It was not just his attitude that had changed; it was his demeanor and the way he held himself. She knew he had a secret. But it was clear to her that he didn't want to share it with anyone yet.

Jared and his dad loaded up the car and headed to their favorite lake for a day of fishing. It was something they both liked to do with each other. It was a "just the guys" thing.

As the guys fished, Stephany went to her mom and told her that Jared was acting strange. "In what way? How is he acting?" Heather asked.

"As though he is keeping a secret," Stephany replied. "But I don't know what it is."

"I noticed the same thing," Heather agreed. "Call it mother's intuition. Are you and your sister ready for your week-long camping trip with the neighbors?"

"Almost, Mom. I just have a few more things to pack, and then I'll be ready."

"Good. Just don't wait until the last minute to get everything packed."

"I won't, but Anna probably will. She hasn't even started packing yet."

"Anna!" Heather yelled. Anna came into the kitchen, and Heather told her she needed to get all her things packed for the camping trip.

"I'll have it done by this afternoon," Anna glumly replied.

But Heather knew that Anna was the procrastinator out of

the two twins. So, she told Anna to go pack immediately.

Grudgingly, Anna replied, "Okay." Then, she went into her room and slammed the door. She turned on her music and stayed in her room for the rest of the afternoon so that her mom would think she was packing her things. But she wasn't packing at all.

Stephany wanted to go fishing with the boys but had not been invited. She remembered her dad saying it was just for men—just like the yard work. She didn't think it was fair that Jared got to spend so much time with their dad and she didn't. She was jealous.

Chapter 2

The Sight

A FTER A LONG DAY of fishing, Jared and Dave finally made it home. It was 3 p.m., and they had both received a lot of sun from the hot summer day. Jared was exhausted, but they had caught their limit of fish. Throughout the day, his mind was preoccupied with the green rock. At one point, he almost lost his pole because he was not paying attention. His dad tried to start conversations with him the whole day, but Jared was too far off in his own thoughts.

When Jared and Dave pulled up to the house, Heather met them outside. She asked Jared how the fishing was, and his only reply was a curt, "Fine." He walked straight into the house, went right to his room, and shut and locked the door behind him.

Heather and Dave looked at each other with bewilderment. Dave shrugged his shoulders and said Jared had been that way the entire day, with his head in the clouds. He was concerned about Jared. "Maybe he has a crush on a girl he can't stop thinking about," was the only thing Dave could proffer. "I can't think of any other reason he would have been so preoccupied while fishing."

"I've noticed something different about him as well," Heather confirmed.

"So, I'm not imagining it?"

"No. Everyone in the house has noticed Jared has changed somehow. We just don't know what caused it. It's like he changed overnight."

Jared was in his room. He had moved the mysterious green object into the center of the room by sliding it out of his closet with his feet so that he wouldn't touch it with his bare hands. The object was sitting there in the middle of a pile of clothes. Jared couldn't see much glow about it, but there was a lot of light coming into his room from the sun. The stone looked almost fluorescent with the sunlight shining on it. Jared was mesmerized by its appearance.

Jared wanted to test whether the things he thought he saw overnight were really there or he had just dreamed them. He knew he needed to touch the object, but he remembered that the last time he did, he got a shock that startled him. After sitting on his bed for a while, he finally got the nerve to walk over to the stone and pick it up. As he leaned down to put his hands around it, he was prepared for another shock. Just as Jared's hands were about to make contact with the object, there was a loud banging at his bedroom door. "Just a minute!" he called out.

After quickly covering up the egg with some clothes, Jared unlocked the door and opened it. There stood Stephany, wanting to know what Jared was hiding. She pushed her way past him and kicked the covered-up egg as she stumbled into the room. Stephany pulled the clothes away and laid her eyes on the fluorescent-looking green rock that was shaped like an egg. "What is that green thing?" she asked with a puzzled look.

Jared quickly shut his bedroom door as he tried to think of a response to Stephany's question. Noticing that Stephany was reaching down to pick the object up, he yelled, "Don't touch it!"

The sudden outburst from Jared made Stephany jump and made her even more curious. She asked again, "What is this thing?"

Not wanting to alert their parents, in a quieter voice, Jared said to Stephany, "Just sit down, and I will tell you what I know about it."

Stephany sat down on Jared's unmade bed, looked directly at him, and said, "Okay, so what is it?"

Jared pulled in a deep breath and emphasized that Stephany could not tell anyone about the mysterious object. She promised him she would keep it a secret, and she looked sincere. So, Jared began his explanation. "Last night, during the storm, I got up because of the lightning and thunder."

Stephany immediately interrupted, saying, "I *knew* you were up!"

"Keep your voice down," Jared reminded his sister in a whisper. Then, he leaned in closer and continued his story. Jared told Stephany everything, even about the cut on his arm and the visions he got while touching the egg-looking thing.

Stephany stared at Jared in disbelief. "So, you're saying that if I touch it, I will get some sort of superpower?" she asked.

"No, don't be silly." Jared went on with his story, finishing with how he was about to experiment with touching the object again just before Stephany knocked on the door.

"Well, then . . . do it!" Stephany urged.

Jared took note of the time. His bedside alarm clock said 3:17 p.m. He walked to the middle of the room and bent down to pick up the egg. As his hands got close to it, they began moving slower, reflecting a renewed hesitation in Jared.

"Oh, just do it already, you coward!" Stephany blurted out.

Jared again reminded Stephany to keep her voice down. As he was about to connect with the object, he could feel its pull again, almost like it was calling him. He looked up at Stephany and asked her if she felt anything different in the room. She wrinkled her brows and responded with, "No." But Jared could feel the electricity in the room—so much so that the hairs on his arms were standing on end.

Stephany noticed the hair standing up on Jared's arm and moved closer to get a better look. As she got closer to Jared and the egg, suddenly, the hair on her head flew straight up as though it had been rubbed on a balloon. She laughed with amazement and repeated, "What *is* this thing, Jared?"

Jared took a deep breath and finally lowered his hands the rest of the way. The instant he grabbed the object, he had the same electric feeling he felt the first time he had touched it. He put both hands around it and stood up. Then, he walked over to his bed with the object in his hands and sat down. Jared told Stephany to sit next to him.

The feeling Jared had this time differed from the first time he had touched the object. The electric feeling did not hurt like it did the first time, but he could still sense it was there. He asked Stephany, "Can you feel the change in the air *now*?"

"Yes," Stephany confirmed. "It feels like there is electricity in the air. Where did this thing come from?"

"It appeared—landed, I suppose—in the backyard last night during the storm. It's what made the hole in the yard."

"That was a big hole it made," Stephany pointed out.

"Yes. I was in the kitchen when it landed in the ground. The green glow from the egg was so bright when it landed that it lit up the kitchen. I thought it was lightning at first, but then, the glow didn't go away the way lightning does."

"What do you think the designs on the side of it are?"

"I don't know, Stephany. I haven't been around this thing much longer than you have. But the markings must mean something, right?"

As Jared and Stephany admired the object, it continued to shine a beautiful green. Stephany was in awe of the lit-up egg. She reached out and finally placed her hand on the stone. She immediately felt a shock, and she and Jared realized they could hear each other's voices in their heads, even without them speaking. All they had to do was think of what they wanted to say, and the other person could hear it.

Without even opening her mouth, Stephany asked Jared, "Can you hear me?"

"Yes, Stephany, I can hear you . . . in my head! This is the coolest thing I've ever experienced." Suddenly, they both looked to the left side of the room. "Did you see that as well?" Jared asked his sister.

"Yes! I saw something move, but there is nothing there."

"The same thing happened to me last night," Jared informed her.

Jared and Stephany continued to hold the egg, continued to hear each other's thoughts, and continued seeing things out of the corner of their eyes. But each time they looked in the direction of the motion, nothing was there. Until eventually, a new world began to appear. It was out of focus at first, but they could both see it. They could see blurred images of people and magical creatures, but no one seemed to see Jared and Stephany.

"Am I really seeing this?" Stephany wondered within Jared's head.

"Yes, you are, Stephany," Jared confirmed. "I see it, too!"

The longer the two were in contact with the egg, the more everything they saw came into focus. Soon, the people who were around them in this other world were looking at Jared and Stephany as the siblings held the green egg. This new attention made Jared and Stephany nervous. So, they placed the egg on the bed and let it go. At once, the mysterious new world disappeared like it had never been there.

Jared covered the egg with his blanket. He left the room with Stephany, and they walked to the kitchen. There, Dave and Heather asked where they had been for the last two hours. Jared and Stephany looked at each other with confusion since they knew they had only been in Jared's room for maybe fifteen minutes. But when they looked at the clock on the kitchen wall, it read 5:08 p.m. Stephany replied that they had been in Jared's room and must have lost track of time.

Before dinner, Jared and Stephany left the kitchen and retreated to a hallway to discuss what was going on. Jared suggested that maybe when the other world is visible, they are in a different time zone where time moves slower. They had only been in contact with the egg for less than ten minutes, but nearly two hours had gone by.

As Jared and Stephany conversed about the green egg, Anna came up from behind them and asked, "What green egg?"

Jared rolled his eyes in annoyance. He didn't want Anna to know anything about the green egg. Nor did Stephany. "It's nothing, Anna," Jared replied with contempt.

But Anna didn't believe him. "Well, if it's nothing, then maybe I'll just go tell Mom and Dad about the magical green egg you're hiding."

Jared panicked, not wanting anyone else to know about the egg. He told Anna that they would let her know about it later that night but that she had to keep it a secret. He told her to bring Stephany to his room after dinner.

Anna agreed but added, "You better be truthful about it tonight, or I *will* let Mom and Dad know."

After dinner, Jared went to his room. Soon after, Anna and Stephany showed up. At dinner, they had told their parents that they were going to be playing a game in Jared's room. Anna tapped her foot impatiently as she waited for Jared to tell her what was going on. And Jared finally pulled his blanket down, revealing the green egg that had been hidden beneath it. The three siblings stared at the stone for a few moments before Anna eventually asked, "Well, what is it?"

Jared repeated the same story he had told Stephany, starting with the storm, and then he added what he and Stephany had experienced with the egg together before dinner. Jared and

Stephany agreed that it would be easiest to just show Anna what happens when they touch the egg. So, Jared picked it up and instantly felt the electric shock. Then, Stephany put her hands on it and told Anna to put her hands on it as well.

As soon as Anna had her hands on the egg, she jumped from the electric shock. Jared had left that part out of his story, so she was not expecting it. The twins could immediately hear what Jared was thinking, which sent them into a fit of giggles. Via their minds, Jared informed Anna that all she needed to do was think about what she wanted to say, and he and Stephany would hear it. They all got the hang of it quickly, and before long, they were having full conversations in their minds.

Anna snapped her head to the right and asked, "Did you guys see that?"

Jared, knowing exactly what Anna was referring to, confirmed, "Yes. Just wait a few more minutes and see what happens."

The siblings all waited patiently as a whole new world slowly came into focus in front of their eyes. Anna appeared to be concerned, but Jared and Stephany reassured her that it would be ok. Everything came into focus much faster this time. Before the trio knew it, people from the other world were clearly standing around looking at them.

Jared kept hold of the egg longer this time than the last two times so he could see what would happen. Along with the people the siblings were seeing, they saw little flying things that looked like fairies. And the people looked different than the people in the world they knew. The people in this new world were not like humans. They were a little shorter and had pointy ears like elf ears, and they all had brilliant and beautiful blue eyes.

The siblings could not believe that an entirely different world existed right on top of their own world. Jared suggested that they put the egg down and let it go so they could discuss what to do next. The twins agreed, and they all set the egg on the bed and lifted their hands off it. The new world disappeared immediately.

Jared looked at his alarm clock and noticed that nearly three hours had gone by this time. It was 9 p.m. As the siblings all walked out of Jared's room, Jared reminded the twins to keep everything about the egg a secret. They returned to the kitchen, where their parents were drinking coffee.

Dave asked his children whether they enjoyed the game. The trio all nodded their heads. "Yes, it was fun!" Anna said with a little too much enthusiasm. Then, Heather asked everyone if they wanted ice cream and hot pudding for dessert, and they all agreed that it sounded great. They spent the rest of the night in the kitchen with each other's company.

At 10 p.m., Dave reminded everyone that it was time for bed. They finished their dessert, cleaned their dishes, and went to their rooms for the night. As the three siblings stared silently at each other, Jared put a finger to his lips to remind them to stay quiet about the egg. Then, they said goodnight to each other and went to their rooms.

Back in his room, Jared could not help himself. He uncovered the egg and held it in his hands. This time, the invisible world appeared faster than before. This was going to be another experiment. As soon as everything was in focus and everyone could see and hear each other, Jared raised a hand to wave at them. The people from the other world followed suit and waved back at him. They seemed friendly. So, Jared asked, "Can you understand me?" The people all nodded their heads yes but didn't say a word.

When Jared asked the people whether they could talk, a girl walked up to him and said, "Hello, I'm Emera. What is your name?"

"Jared," he replied.

A knock on Jared's door startled him. It was his dad telling him to go to sleep because, by then, it was 1:00 in the morning. When Jared heard the knock, he had let go of the egg and thrown it under his covers. He had forgotten about the time disparities when he had picked up the egg. It was now clear that there was a time difference and that when the two worlds were connected, time went by slower in the new world than in Jared's world.

Jared set the egg on his dresser, covered it with a shirt, and got into bed. That night, he dreamed about Emera and how beautiful she was. She was the essence of what he figured a mystical princess would look like: long glowing golden hair, blue eyes to match any ocean, tan skin, and little pointy ears. She wore a gown made of jewels and sequins that seemed to change colors as she moved and talked. In Jared's dream, he and Emera were talking and getting to know each other. She was the princess in her world. And Jared saw that there were many magical creatures in her world—both good and bad creatures. The fairies that Jared saw flying around were friends of the people in Onteria. That was the name of their world.

Jared woke up early in the morning, remembering his dream like it had really happened. That's how it felt to him— real. When Jared sat up in bed, he looked over at his dresser and noticed that the egg was missing. He panicked for a minute but then felt something right next to him in bed. It was the egg. So, did he merely dream about speaking with Emera in Onteria, or had it really happened? Jared couldn't remember getting up and bringing the green egg to bed. He was extremely confused.

The last thing Jared remembered was putting the egg on his dresser. So, how did it get into his bed? As he pondered that question, he got up and went to get breakfast in the kitchen. When his dad greeted him there and asked him what he had been doing up so late, Jared fibbed that he was just talking to himself because he couldn't sleep.

"Who is Emera?" Dave asked.

Dave's question startled Jared, and Jared noticed that his mother seemed startled as well. Jared responded, "How do you know that name?"

"I heard you saying it out loud last night. So, I went into your room, and you were asleep but talking out loud about someone named Emera."

Jared blew it off like it was no one he knew. "I must have been dreaming, is all."

"Well, it must have been a pleasant dream because you were talking all night."

Jared did not say anything else. He just sheepishly sat at the kitchen table and ate his breakfast. He did wonder why his mother startled at the name Emera, though.

While Jared ate breakfast, he heard soft voices coming

from all around him. He thought someone was calling his name, so he asked, "What?"

Dave and Heather looked at Jared with confusion. "We didn't say anything, honey," his mom informed him.

Jared found that odd because he knew what he heard was real. Then, out of the corner of his left eye, he thought he saw Emera. He knew it was her from her glowing golden hair flowing in the wind and the clothes that were covered in jewels and changed colors as she moved. Jared shifted his vision to the left, and yes, there he saw her. Emera was standing on the other side of the kitchen.

"What are you looking at so intently?" Jared's dad asked.

Since Jared was sure his mom and dad could not see Emera, he had to make up an excuse. He told him he was not looking at anything, just tired and staring off. He went back to his breakfast and now devoured it as fast as he could. His mom told him to slow down or he might choke on his food.

When Jared finished eating, he rinsed off his dishes and returned to his room, where he could see more Onterians every place he looked. Emera was there and said, "Hello." But Jared froze and didn't know what to say.

Realizing he was not touching the green egg, Jared stammered out, "How is it that I am able to see you?"

Emera informed Jared that the green device that had landed in his backyard was called an Incognal. Interacting with it opens one's eyes to other worlds—worlds like Onteria. After a person touches the Incognal for long enough, they gain the ability to choose to see other worlds whenever they please, without its help.

Jared thought about how he woke up with the Incognal in his bed without remembering how it go there. "Do you know how the Incognal ended up in bed with me last night?"

"Yes," Emera responded. "I placed it there. Once I discovered your world, I was able to see it whenever I chose to. So, I chose to last night, and I moved the Incognal."

Jared had many questions. "This Incognal . . . did it come from *your* world?"

"No. It came from the universe. And it chose to land in your backyard for you to find it. The universe doesn't make mistakes. You were destined to find the Incognal, and I'm glad you did."

Jared tried to make further conversation with Emera, but he didn't know what to say. He was flustered by Emera's beauty and by the strange circumstances he found himself in. Every time he spoke, he would jumble the first few words into an incoherent sentence.

Emera laughed at Jared. She could tell he was nervous and not used to being around exquisite girls. "There are few of my kind of people left in Onteria. So, some of them left Onteria and asked the universe for help—for us to survive. In response, the universe sent you to us, Jared."

Jared did not know what to say at that point. He stared at Emera with a dumbfounded look and asked, "What do you mean?"

"My people have been around for thousands of years, Jared. But there are no longer enough men in our world. The women in our society outnumber the men fifteen to one, and the men are mostly having female offspring, not male."

"Yes, ok, but how does this involve me?"

"Because the universe has chosen *you* to help my people survive."

Jared was just as confused as ever and still didn't know what to say. "Can we just be, like, um . . . *friends*?"

"Yes, Jared. I have been waiting for you for a long time."

That answer made Jared bashfully reply, "Why have you been waiting for me?"

"The universe has betrothed us to each other."

"What do you mean?" Jared asked sheepishly.

"The universe has sent you to me. Our families have always been intended to be together."

"How do you know about my family?"

"I have known your family for hundreds of years."

Jared was beginning to think Emera might be crazy. "I am only seventeen years old. If you're talking about marriage, I'm too young for that."

"Well, I'm 119 years old, and I have been waiting patiently for you all these years." Emera spoke in a soft voice that Jared felt was very calming. "We will discuss this further. For now, anytime you want to see me, just think of me, and I will be here." With that, Emera vanished as though she had never been there.

Jared's mom knocked on his bedroom door. "Are you gonna be in there all day, Jared?"

Looking at the clock on his bedside table, Jared saw that it was already 1:00 in the afternoon. He continued to be shocked and thrown off by the time shifts when his world converged with Onteria. He got dressed for the day.

When Jared exited his room, his dad intercepted him and said they needed to talk. Dave was convinced that Jared's sudden change in demeanor was all about a new girl at school. Whenever Jared's parents wanted to have a serious talk with him, they would take him out for ice cream. So, Jared, his mom, and his dad loaded into the family car and left the house.

"So, why are we going to get ice cream this time," Jared asked.

"We need to have a talk about girls," Dave informed his son.

"I repeat: WHY?"

"Because we know your secret."

"You know?!" Jared was disappointed, thinking his parents had discovered the egg.

"Yes, Jared. We know you've met a girl and that you're changing. We can all see the change in you, even the twins."

"Your entire persona has changed, seemingly overnight," Heather added. "I can see that your aura is running hot." Heather always said she could see people's auras. Jared usually didn't believe here, but this time, she was right. He was feeling happy about meeting a girl.

When they got to the ice cream shop and ordered their ice cream, Jared and his parents sat at the same table they always did. Jared's parents looked at him and smiled. Eventually, Heather said, "As your father mentioned, we noticed you've been acting strange for at least a couple of days now, and we think we know why. It's a girl, isn't it?"

"Yes . . . I mean, no . . . I mean, it's complicated. You wouldn't understand." Jared was already beginning to feel foolish for engaging his parents on the matter.

"Try us," Dave insisted.

Jared instead just sat in silence and waited for his ice cream to arrive. As he saw the ice cream coming, he told his parents he had nothing left to say about it. But Heather continued to pry right up until the ice cream arrived. "Do you know how to kiss a girl?" she asked.

"Stop! I don't have a girlfriend. And yes, I already know all about that stuff."

"Well, if you ever need to talk about it, just let us know. We're always here for you," Dave offered.

"Can you at least tell us her name?" Heather asked.

Without thinking, Jared blurted out, "Emera!"

Heather went quiet for a moment and then repeated, "Emera."

"Yes. I met her just the other day. I'm done talking about her now." Jared finished his ice cream in silence and didn't say another word before they returned home.

When Jared and his parents got home, he vanished into his bedroom, looking forward to some peace and privacy. But Stephany walked right in behind him. "Ice cream, huh?" she teased, knowing it meant a serious talk with their parents.

"Yep. Ice cream it was," Jared confirmed.

Stephany turned her thoughts to the Incognal. "Have you used the green thingy again recently?" Jared shook his head no. "Okay," was all Stephany said before walking out of the room and shutting the door behind her.

Remembering what Emera had told him, Jared shut his eyes and thought about her, hoping to summon her to his room.

He reopened his eyes, and a whole new world appeared before him. He was still amazed he could do that even without touching the Incognal. And sure enough, Emera was right there in front of him, too. "Hello, Jared," she greeted him. "It's so good to see you again."

Jared smiled at Emera. "So, can I travel *into* your world?" Jared asked. "Or am I just stuck here looking at it through my bedroom walls?"

Without a word, Emera walked up to Jared and held out her hand for him to take. As soon has Jared put his hand in hers, his world disappeared, and he was standing in Onteria. "Who are you here?" Jared asked. "I mean, what is it you do here?"

"I am a princess—Princess Emera of Onteria."

Jared could not believe what he had heard. "Wait a second; you're a *princess*? And you've been waiting for *me*?" He laughed out loud. He had never known a real princess before. He had only seen them on TV. "I thought a princess has to marry a prince."

Emera turned her face toward Jared's and smiled as they continued to walk. As they were walking, little fairies were flying around them. One even landed on Jared's shoulder and whispered in his ear. He looked at Emera and said, "I can hear it talking to me."

"Yes, all the creatures of this world can speak if you will just listen."

The fairy was telling Jared to say hello to his mother for it. Jared did not understand why it would tell him to do that. Then, Jared noticed an even larger flying thing in the sky.

"You look frightened," Emera said.

Once Jared had caught his breath, he said, "I'm more confused than frightened. What is that thing flying right over us?" The thing was not as big as a dragon but maybe about a quarter the size of one. It had long feathers with vibrant colors of red and yellow, and it had a large beak that looked like and alligator's mouth.

"That is what you, in your world, would call a bird," Emera informed Jared. "But to us, it is called a muse. They are good luck. And they are attracted to one person their entire lifetime. They will follow that person wherever they go until the muse dies. That one above us has followed me around for over one hundred years."

"It's beautiful. And it flies so gracefully for something so big," Jared noted.

"Yes, they are meant to be in the air, just to keep watch on their one chosen person."

Emera took Jared to her palace. It was beautifully adorned with colors and jewels of all kinds. The floor changed colors as they walked on it. The grand entrance they walked through was at least twenty feet tall. And the lights around them were different jewels that glowed so brightly you could see your shadow on the wall.

"How do those glow so bright?" Jared asked.

"They are magic stones," Emera explained. "They begin glowing as soon as they are brought out from the mountain and exposed to our sun. After that, they will glow forever. They are also what power our cities. Some stones can generate great power and others just enough to light up a small room."

Jared looked amazed. He had only seen things like this in science fiction movies. Emera gave him a ring to wear that had a very shiny crystal in it. She said, "This stone will help protect you if you ever get into trouble."

"Wow! This ring is incredible. It looks like something a prince would wear."

Emera smiled at Jared and told him that the stones people wear change colors depending on how the person feels at any given moment. "Blue means happy, and yellow means excited," Emera informed Jared. "And red means you are feeling unhappy or mad." As Jared and Emera walked along together, hand in hand, both of their colors were blue but with a yellow design within the stone. They were both happy and excited at that moment.

Jared looked Emera right in the eyes and said to her, "The first time I saw you, your eyes were an ocean blue. But now, they are a yellowish green. Why is that?"

"There are many things in Onteria that change depending on how people feel. The resting color of our eyes is blue, but they change depending on the occasion."

"What does green mean?"

"It is the color of love."

Jared blushed as soon as Emera said that. Emera just smiled. And they kept on walking. But eventually, Jared told Emera he needed to get back to his world. They had been walking around Onteria for well over an hour, so Jared knew he must have been gone for much longer than that in his world.

As Jared walked with Emera back to his world, he saw many different animals and people. Everyone was very nice and welcoming to him. One animal he saw really intrigued him. It was called a rock dragon and seemed to be the size of a small cat. Like the muses, rock dragons also attached themselves to only one person and were like a personal alarm system. They could sense danger close by and warn you. Emera explained that the rock dragons were found mostly in mountain tunnels, and if you ever find one and give it a treat, it will follow you forever. "Just don't get them mad, though," Emera warned Jared. They can be vicious little creatures!"

Emera led Jared back to the location of his home. As soon as she let go of his hand, he could see both worlds again, one on top of the other. Jared and Emera said their goodbyes to each other, and Emera said, "I hope to see you again soon." Then, Onteria vanished, and Jared was alone in his room.

When Jared left his room, he was dismayed to discover that his entire family was in a panic and had even called the police to their home. Jared had been missing without a trace for over seven hours. His mom ran over to him and hugged him, with tears rolling down her face.

Dave looked angry but also concerned. "Where have you been?" he asked.

"Just in my room!" Jared replied. He honestly wasn't sure whether the words he spoke were true or not. He had *kind of* been there.

Everyone immediately jumped on Jared at once, explaining that they had searched his room several times and he wasn't there. Even the police had checked his room, they explained. He definitely had not been there.

Jared had to think of something quick, so he made up a story. He knew he couldn't tell them he had been in an alternate world caused by a green stone he found one stormy night. So, he told them he climbed out his bedroom window to meet a girl and lost track of time.

The police looked at Dave and Heather and said, "This is a family matter now. We'll leave it in your hands." Then, they left the house. But not before warning Jared that the next time he disappeared like that, he would be in trouble with them.

Jared's parents told him to sit down at the kitchen table and tell them everything. Jared agreed and said that the girl's name was Emera and that he had just met her the other day. Jared's parents were mad at him, but as soon as they were told it was a girl, they calmed down and were just glad that he was home safe. His dad told him they were going to have another talk the next day, and this time about a green stone. But now, it was the middle of the night and time for everyone to go to bed.

Jared went back to his room and put the Incognal back in his closet, covering the stone with some clothes. But he wondered how his dad had found out about it. Jared decided that the next time he went to Onteria, he would need to be careful about the stone and keep better track of time.

Jared went to bed and fell fast asleep even though he had not been that tired. Just before getting into bed, he was still wired from his trip to Onteria. It had been an exciting trip and one he knew he would never forget. That night, he dreamed about Emera and how beautiful she was and her world, Onteria, was. It allowed him to sleep peacefully.

Back in the kitchen, Heather told Dave that she needed to be alone for a while to think. "Think about what?" Dave inquired.

"About who this girl is. This . . . Emera."

Dave felt that his wife said the name Emera as though she knew the person. But he disregarded it, gave his wife a kiss, and told her not to stay up too late. He reminded her that she would need to get the twins off on their camping trip in the morning.

Chapter 3

Secret

AFTER A GOOD NIGHT of sleep, Jared woke up feeling better than he had in a long time. When he went to the kitchen to have breakfast, his mom asked him if he was feeling alright. "Yes. Why?" he replied.

"You just look full of color, energetic, and even like you've gained some muscle tone. Have you been working out?"

"No, I haven't. But yes, I feel good today."

Heather asked Jared about the new ring he was wearing. Jared explained that Emera had given it to him and that it was a good luck charm and would protect him. "It's an exquisite ring," Heather noted. "I had one like it when I was young." Jared thought that comment was strange, considering that the ring had come from an entirely different world.

Jared was indeed looking more muscular than usual, and he had a glow to him that he had never had before. When he was leaving the kitchen, his dad reminded him, "This afternoon, we're going to have that talk about the green stone you found."

Jared scurried out of the room but could still hear his mom and dad talking in the kitchen. "It must be some girl," he heard Dave say. "Don't worry; I'll talk to him soon."

As Jared sat in his room, he began daydreaming about Onteria. He wanted to visit there again, but he couldn't because everyone at home was watching him. If he disappeared again, he might find himself in big trouble. But he figured he could probably see Emera without actually entering her world.

When Jared thought about Emera, suddenly, Onteria appeared. But he didn't see Emera. Instead, there was an older man standing before Jared. And Jared could tell that this man didn't like him much since his eyes were red in color. Jared remembered what Emera had told him about the color changes and what they meant.

The old man spoke, saying, "I am Sadean, and I will be married to the princess. You are not welcome here."

Jared was confused. Emera told him he was brought to her by the universe and that she had been waiting for him for over one hundred years. So, he did not understand what Sadean was saying. "Where is Emera?" Jared asked.

"She will never speak with you again," Sadean affirmed.

Jared didn't believe that, so he pushed Sadean harder to find out where Emera was. But this made Sadean angry, and he moved close enough to Jared to grab Jared's arm and pull him into Onteria. Jared tried to break free of Sadean's grip, but he was too strong—a lot stronger than Jared. Sadean said, "One last time, you are not welcome here . . . unless *you* want to be my prisoner as well."

Jared finally broke free from Sadean's grip, and Onteria

joined up with Jared's world again. Jared thought very hard about his own world in order to move away from Onteria, and suddenly, Onteria completely vanished. Jared was back in his room.

Jared sensed that Emera was in trouble and that he needed to save her. He just didn't know how. He knew he could not call to her or else Sadean might show up, and he was the last person Jared wanted to see. *Maybe if I just hold the Incognal in my hands*, Jared thought, *Onteria will appear, and I can try to get someone else there to help me save the princess.*

Jared went to his closet to get the Incognal, but he was distraught to discover that the stone was gone. His heart sank. He rushed out of his room and went around the house, asking if anyone had been in his room.

Jared's parents reminded him that they had all recently been in his room, and the cops had, too. Heather asked him why he wanted to know so badly. Since Jared knew he couldn't tell them the real reason, he said, "Because I'm missing the game I was playing with Anna and Stephany the other night." At this point, he was beginning to panic and was out of breath.

Heather told Jared to calm down and said, "Maybe if you clean your room once in a while, you'll find whatever it is you're looking for."

Jared simply grunted in response and went looking for the green egg in other places. *Maybe Stephany took it*, he thought. So, he went to her room, but she wasn't there. He next tried Anna's room, but she wasn't there either. When Jared asked his parents where the twins had gone, his mother reminded him that they had left for a camping trip with the neighbor girls.

"Don't you remember, Jared? They have been planning this trip for the last month."

Jared had forgotten about the camping trip. With all the crazy things happening around him, time had gotten away from him. So, he simply said, "Okay. Yeah, I remember." Then, he went back to his room in a hurry.

Once back in his room, Jared began pacing back and forth. He needed to know where the Incognal had gone. He figured one of his sisters must have taken it on their camping trip. The thought of that made Jared start to feel nauseous since he knew it could be dangerous for them with Sadean lurking around and making threats.

Without the Incognal, Jared knew he had to come up with a different plan for helping Emera. He hoped that once his parents went to bed, he could try contacting her again directly. But for now, he knew his dad was coming to talk to him about the green stone. And sure enough, just then, there was a knock on Jared's bedroom door. "Can I come in?" Dave asked.

"Yes," Jared replied.

Jared's dad entered the room and shut the door behind him. He took a seat in the desk chair, and the father and son sat silently staring at each other for a few moments. Finally, Dave said, "So, can you tell me about the green stone I heard about?"

Jared knew there was no point in denying the stone existed. So, he asked, "How did you hear about the stone?"

"I just . . . heard about it. Let's leave it at that."

"And what do you want to know?"

"I want to know why you lied to me about the hole in the yard."

41

"Fine. I'll tell you the entire story," Jared agreed.

"I heard it's magical," Dave prodded.

Jared took a deep breath and started at the beginning. It took about thirty minutes for him to tell the entire story; there was a lot to tell. As soon as Jared got to the point where he was gone for seven hours, his dad stopped him and said, "Okay, I've heard enough. Enough with the magic green stone thing. It's time you tell me the truth. What *really* happened when you disappeared?"

"I *am* telling you the truth, Dad. You've got to believe me," Jared implored. But he knew it would be hard to convince his dad of that now that the stone was missing. "I want to show you how the Incognal . . . I mean, the stone works. But I can't find it. The girls must have taken it on their camping trip."

"No, they didn't take it. I have it," Dave revealed. "I found it in the back of your closet this morning while you were eating breakfast."

"What were you doing in my room?"

"I was looking for drugs because you've changed. You've changed your appearance, you're more defiant, and you're sneaking out of the house for hours at a time."

Jared went quiet for a moment but then blurted out, "You have no right to go through my things! I'm not on drugs. It's the stone that's changed me. And it's called an Incognal, by the way."

Dave went to his room, retrieved the stone, and set it in front of Jared. "Prove it to me, son. Show me how it works."

Jared took the Incognal in his hands. But this time, he felt no shock. He was holding the stone tight, but nothing was happening. He was getting frustrated with it. Jared put the stone down on his bed while his dad sat there with a disappointed look on his face.

Dave stood up and said, "You're grounded until you can tell me the truth." Then, he walked out of the room.

"But I *am* telling the truth!" Jared yelled after his father.

Jared was confused and frustrated by the Incognal not working. He decided to give it another try. This time, as soon as he touched it, the Incognal gave him a shock and glowed brighter than ever. Jared thought this was strange since it had never glowed brighter from him touching it. And this time, when Onteria appeared, there was no one around—another first. All the other times Onteria had appeared, there had been many Onterians around. Jared was determined to find out what was going on.

Jared grabbed a backpack to carry the stone in once he got into the city of Onteria, which was the capital of the Kingdom of Onteria. The longer he held the Incognal, the clearer the city became, and Jared's own world vanished. As soon as he was completely in Onteria, he put the Incognal in his pack. Then, he walked around to see if he could find anyone. But he couldn't see anyone for as far as he could see. There were no people, animals, or bazaars like he had seen on previous trips to Onteria. Everyone was gone!

The weather differed from before, too. The other times Jared had visited Onteria, there had been a beautiful purple sky and an orange sun. But this time, the sky was more reddish, and the sun was almost buried by the color of the sky. Jared said out loud, "I guess *everything* changes from how someone feels. But whose feelings control the weather?"

While Jared was walking around, heading toward the palace Emera had taken him to, he also noticed that the paths of cultured color marble were not turning blue. Instead, the marble was a color that he had never seen before. He wasn't even sure that it was a color at all, but he almost became hypnotized by it. When he finally snapped out of his trance, he continued to walk toward the palace.

Jared could see the palace ahead of him, but no matter how much he walked, it didn't seem to get any closer. In fact, the more he walked, the further away the palace seemed to get. Jared wasn't making much headway. But he noticed that the Incognal was glowing even more now, almost like it was guiding him in the direction it wanted him to go in. *I should give this a test*, Jared thought. He turned around and walked in the opposite direction, and the further he walked in that direction, the less the stone glowed. So, he turned around again, facing the palace, and started walking. The Incognal began to glow again.

The longer Jared held the Incognal, the more he could feel its power. It was more than just a rock that brought a new world into focus; it was attracted to him. *It must be attracted to whomever it's leading me to as well*, Jared thought. He assumed the Incognal was leading him to the princess since it seemed to be trying to take him toward the palace.

Suddenly, a large shadow passed over Jared. He looked up and saw that it was one of those enormous bird-like things. He tried to remember everything Emera had told him about them. *It's called a muse, and it's only attracted to one person*, Jared recalled. *So, why is this one flying around me?*

On this trip to Onteria, Jared made sure to wear a watch. So, he knew he had been walking there for twenty minutes Onterian time—or about an hour back home. Jared knew he needed to keep track of the time so he could get back before his parents worried. But he also felt that he had to find the princess no matter how long that took.

Eventually, Jared saw someone on the horizon. Whoever it was, they were heading right toward him. The closer the unknown individual got to Jared, the more Jared could make out the person's features. It was a man with long black hair, and he was dressed in colorful garb. It looked like he was wearing some kind of robe. But the closer the man got, Jared could tell that it was not a robe on the man's back but a muse. And it's red and yellow feathers draped down around the man like a robe.

The mysterious man got within fifty feet of Jared, and they both stopped. The man was not Sadean; it was someone else. The man called out to Jared, asking him if he was on a quest to save the princess. Jared was quiet for a moment and then said, "Yes!" Just then, the muse that was on the man's back came to life and flew off the man and toward Jared. Jared got nervous. He knew nothing about muses. If they were used for attacking people, he felt he might be in trouble.

The muse landed on Jared's back and swung its wings around him, shielding him like a suit of armor. Jared jumped and let out a shriek, and the mysterious man vanished right in front of his eyes. The feathers on the muse felt hard as steel—like what Jared imagined dragon scales would feel like. The muse surrounded him like a security blanket. At that moment, Jared could feel the power of the muse; it had become part of him.

Jared wondered who the man he had seen was and why he had given him a muse. And why didn't the man go save the princess himself? Jared brushed these questions off and started walking again, keeping the palace in his sight. When he next looked down at his watch, he saw that he had now been in Onteria for a little over thirty minutes—an hour and a half back home. And yet, he didn't seem to be any closer to the palace. His plan was to stay in Onteria for an hour Onterian time, then head home to make sure he was not being searched for again.

The Incognal started vibrating as if it were trying to tell Jared something. He stopped and pointed it in each direction— right, then left, then to his back. The vibration stopped when he pointed it to the left and behind him. So, he traveled to the right, which was the direction the Incognal seemed to be indicating. But that was now taking Jared *away* from the palace. He speculated the princess must be being held someplace other than the palace. But where was she?

Jared found it strange that he had seen no animals other than the muse that was draped around him. It was almost like the other animals were hiding. Then, he realized that for as big as the muse was, he could not even feel the weight of it on his shoulders. If he didn't know it was there, he would have thought that he had nothing on him at all.

A large spire appeared ahead of Jared, but it looked like it was part of a mountain. The closer he got to it, the more he was certain it was where the Incognal was leading him. But this time, he was actually getting closer to the mountain, unlike the palace, which seemed to keep getting further away from him.

There was a cool breeze blowing against Jared, and he could have sworn it smelled like the princess did the first time he met her. It gave him hope that he was going in the right direction and that she was calling him. By then, forty-five minutes had gone by, and Jared still had quite a bit of a distance to cover to reach the spire. The closer Jared got to the mountain, the harder the ground got. It became rockier and dirtier—it was not clean and pretty like it was in the area of the bazaars.

Jared knew he would have to put the Incognal down in fifteen minutes to get back home in time, figuring that setting the stone down would be enough to immediately transport him there. In his heart, he knew he had to keep looking for the princess. But if his parents returned to his room and found him missing again, he wouldn't know how to explain it to them this time.

Jared made it to the spire-like mountain and discovered that there was an entrance at the bottom of the spire. The critical moment had come; he had to decide whether to go home and come back later or just keep going. The longer he stood there, the more anxious he became. He wanted to continue his quest, but he had already been gone from his home for three hours, and he was sure that someone had noticed by now.

To stop the Incognal's effects on him, Jared set it on the ground. But nothing seemed to happen! Jared's world did not appear, and the green glow from the stone got brighter. This worried him a little. He wondered whether he might be stuck in

Onteria forever. He figured that if he were stuck there for now, he might as well continue his journey. He picked up the Incognal and put it back in his pack, and with the muse also still on his back, he headed into the tunnel under the spire.

Back home, Heather stopped off at Jared's room to check on him and was disappointed to find he was not there. She screamed for Dave to come meet her at Jared's bedroom. As soon as he got there, she informed him that his son was gone again. Anger welled up in Dave. He was sure his once obedient son had snuck out the window again. But he didn't know where to look for him. They didn't know anything about the girl except that her name was Emera.

Dave blurted out, "I'm calling the police again!" And despite Heather protesting that it would do no good, just like last time, Dave made the call.

"Hello, this is 911," the operator said. "What is your emergency?"

"My son is missing, and we don't know where he could have gone."

"How long has he been gone?"

"I don't know. Maybe two, three hours. He snuck out through his bedroom window."

"Police are on their way to your location, sir."

When the police arrived, Heather was embarrassed to see it was the same two officers who responded the first time Jared disappeared. They took down a statement from Dave, and then one of the officers informed him that "Until Jared has been missing for over twenty-four hours, there's nothing we can do. But we'll keep an eye out for him." The officers left, and

Heather began to cry. She did not want to lose her son this way, to some forbidden love.

Dave searched Jared's room and realized that the green rock was gone. It made him wonder if maybe Jared had been telling the truth and had vanished into another world. But then, he came to his senses and realized that what Jared had told him was impossibly silly and had to have been made up. It made Dave angry.

Dave went to a nearby hardware store and bought some window locks. The locks required keys to open them, not a combination. Dave installed them on all the windows in Jared's room so that when Jared got home, he couldn't sneak back in with no one knowing. He would have to use the front door.

As Jared's parents looked for him, he found himself in a tunnel that would have been too dark for him to see were it not for the Incognal's glow lighting the way, even from within the backpack. Once Jared was twenty feet into the tunnel, an iron gate went up behind him. He was trapped in the tunnel and didn't even know if it was really leading him to the princess. *Perhaps it's a trap*, Jared thought. He took a deep breath and marched forward, which was the only way he could go.

At the end of the corridor, there was a T intersection, and the Incognal was not giving Jared any clue as to the direction he needed to be going. This would be Jared's first actual decision in Onteria with no help. Right or left? He had to decide.

Jared stood at the juncture of the two paths and finally chose left. He didn't know why he chose that direction, but he felt good about it. He glanced down at his watch and discovered it had stopped working. It last showed he had been away

49

from his home for almost four hours. Jared knew his parents must have noticed that he was gone by now.

As Jared was heading down the green-glowing tunnel, he noticed a set of glowing beady eyes sitting on some rocks. Whatever the eyes belonged to let out a squeak, then it sounded like it was purring like a cat. The thing stepped out of the darkness and was the strangest-looking thing Jared had ever seen. He had a pack of cookies in his pack, so he pulled it out and opened it up. He gave a cookie to the rock dragon, and as soon as he did, it wrapped itself around Jared's leg. The dragon kept on purring, and Jared could feel the vibrations through his pantlegs. He reached down, patted the dragon on the head, and said, "I'm going to call you Olly."

Olly looked like a tiny dragon with small wings. He had two back legs that he could walk on and two front arms with long, retractable claws. Jared thought Olly was kind of cute. So, he told Olly, "I think I'll keep you." Olly looked up at Jared with appreciative eyes as if he understood what was being said. Jared remembered what Emera told him, that most of the animals in Onteria could talk if you would just listen. Jared assumed that if animals like Olly could talk to people, they must be able to understand people as well.

Chapter 4

Decisions

D AVE WAS PACING back and forth as he waited for Jared to come home. Dave and Heather had propped open Jared's bedroom door so that they could hear if anyone tried to come through the windows. Heather was getting anxious; Jared had been gone a long time—longer than he had been gone last time. She had called all his friends to check whether he was at their homes. But none of them had seen Jared or knew anything about this girl named Emera. That upset his parents even more.

Jared tried again to put down the Incognal. This time, he left it on the ground for several minutes. But he got the same results. Nothing happened. He was stuck in the tunnel. As he headed down the left corridor, it seemed to go on forever without changing directions. Since he was unable to return home anyway, he was now determined to see this through to the end and find the princess.

A breeze picked up throughout the tunnel, and it carried Emera's scent to Jared again. He knew he was going in the right direction. But suddenly, he heard a voice he recognized. It was Sadean, and he was standing about twenty feet in front of Jared. Jared could feel the feathers of the muse tighten up around his body as Sadean got closer as if the muse sensed that Sadean meant harm toward Jared.

Jared yelled out, "Stop!" The men were now ten feet away from each other. Sadean had a muse on him as well, but his was black with red mixed in. Jared's was still red with yellow mixed into it. Jared felt uneasy about the way Sadean's muse looked. It looked like it wanted to eat Jared. But Jared knew his muse was there to protect him with its life.

Sadean pulled out a sword and held it in the air in a manner making it clear that he was skilled at using it. Suddenly, the Incognal turned into a brilliant silver and green sword with a gold hilt. Sadean took one looked at it, put his sword down, and said, "It looks like you have some help on your side." The next thing Jared knew, Sadean was walking backward until he seemed to vanish. That is something Jared could not get used to——people in Onteria just disappearing like it was a normal thing.

The Incognal turned back into its normal egg-like shape and glowed bright enough that Jared could see a great distance down the dark tunnel. Another iron gate sprung up behind him, just like the first one did. He was surely locked in until he found the princess. But what other tricks did Sadean have up his sleeve?

Jared knew the Incognal was more than just a shiny green rock; it was a living thing. He could hear some growling down the tunnel, coming from somewhere past where he could see.

He knew it was something dangerous. The muse that had been draped around him was no longer on his back. It had now gotten in front of him. It was moving slowly forward and emanating its own low growl, along with a piercing screech every few seconds. It seemed to be using its echo to locate the danger ahead.

Jared's new dragon friend, Olly, wasn't purring anymore. It was in front of him as well, with all its claws out and fully extended and with its wings fully erect to its sides. Both Olly and the muse were now too far in front of Jared for him to see them anymore.

Soon, the growling from the unknown creature in the dark end of the tunnel got more intense. Jared realized that the other creature was using echoes to locate his muse just as his muse was doing. As the echoes got closer to each other, Jared could see that a fight was inevitable. Suddenly, there was the sound of clanging metal. Jared assumed the sound was from the stiff feathers of two muses clashing together. His muse was in a fight for its life, all to protect Jared. Jared could not make out exactly what was happening, though, until both animals came bounding out of the dark tunnel wrapped around each other with their talons out. The black muse Jared had seen with Sadean was on top of Jared's red one and had it by the throat.

The color of Jared's muse was changing to green and red. He didn't know what that meant, but he watched as it also grew bigger. Within minutes, Jared's muse was almost double the size of the black muse, and it now had the black muse by the chest and throat. Jared's muse tore the heart out of the black muse, and Jared could see that the heart was glowing. His muse ate it in one bite, and then his muse's color changed back to red and yellow, and its size went back to normal. His muse took to the air and returned to its perch on Jared's back, draping its feathers around Jared's body.

Olly gave a loud screech and began pointing behind Jared with his wing. Jared felt something hit his back, but it didn't seem to faze the muse. Jared turned around and found himself face-to-face with Sadean. Sadean had attacked from the back, striking with his sword. Jared barely felt it because of the armor he had around him, but he heard it because of the sound of metal on metal. Instantly, Jared had a sword in his hands, and it was blocking each blow that came at him from Sadean. Jared didn't know how to use a sword, so he was amazed when he moved like a trained swordsman. Then, his attacker vanished as fast as he had appeared. It was a blitz attack. Jared wondered if this was how Sadean fought, striking before Jared's defenses were ready.

Jared advanced through the tunnel, but it seemed to have no end. Then, another gate appeared, this time in front of him. The only way forward was through the gate, but Jared couldn't see where it led. Olly rejoined Jared and the muse, wrapping around Jared's leg and purring again.

By now, Jared had been gone from home for over five hours. Dave and Heather were worried sick. Their anger had changed to concern and fear that something bad might have happened to Jared. Dave expected him back well before now, thinking Jared had only left to blow off some steam.

Jared heard voices in the distance, but they were not ones he had heard before. The voices' owners finally came into view, and there were three of them. The muse didn't seem to mind these three, so Jared acknowledged them with a wave, and they returned the gesture. The leader of the group was named Hurstle, and he was with Jonaria and Ferulous. He introduced the three of them to Jared and said, "We are on a quest to save the princess. Will you join us?"

"My name is Jared. And I'm also on a quest to find the princess. Yes, I will join you," Jared happily agreed.

Olly jumped off Jared's leg, went up to Hurstle, and jumped onto his shoulder as if to say hello. Hurstle said, "Well, hello, my little friend. It's good to see you again." Jonaria handed Olly a fig, and he ate the entire thing in one bite.

Jared's three companions looked down at the Incognal in his hands and told him that he was a lucky man to have gained the trust of the Incognal spirit. Jared didn't know what they meant by that, but he was happy to be with other people who seemed to be on his side. "What do you mean by the Incognal spirit?" he inquired.

The three strangers explained that the Incognal was a free-roaming spirit that lives throughout the universe; it does not belong to any one single person unless it chooses them. Incognals are very rare, they explained. And when an Incognal is found by someone, it attaches itself to that person for life. That is why evil practitioners seek them out. But unless someone gains its trust, the Incognal remains just a green rock.

Jared's three new companions went on to explain that the Incognal spirit is the spirit of a deceased king or queen of Onteria. "This one must be an ancestor of Princess Emera or one of our more recent leaders, or else it would not have brought you to help her," Ferulous noted. "If the Incognal spirit trusts you enough, one day it might reveal its true self to you."

"Incognals can be good or bad, though," Jonaria added. "You can usually tell by looking at the color. A green glow is only apparent when the Incognal's finder is pure and not evil. But if someone is dark, an Incognal changes to red. Sometimes an Incognal will start green, but when its finder turns bad, the Incognal will turn from green to a glowing red."

"How did you come across an Incognal that trusts you enough to protect you?" Ferulous asked.

"It landed in my backyard on a stormy night, and I found it there," Jared explained.

"There is no happenstance with an Incognal spirit," Ferulous replied. "They *choose* who they want to find them. And this one has chosen you, my friend."

Jared was dumbfounded by what he was hearing. "I don't even know how to use it," he said in an uncertain voice.

"Once the Incognal has linked with its host, all the host needs to do is think about what they want, and the Incognal does the rest. Or, if it feels its host is in danger, the Incognal will act on its own."

Jared paused and thought for a moment, then said, "So, that's why it became a sword when I needed one! But why is it no longer letting me go home when I set it down?"

Hurstle jumped in with, "A connection has already been made. You no longer need to be touching it for it to protect or assist you. And it will obey your wishes. If you really want to go home, then it will take you home. If it's not taking you home, then you must have other desires—a desire to stay here."

Hurstle noticed that Jared also had a muse and a dragon to aid in his quest. He pointed out that it is very rare to see an outsider with an Incognal, a muse, and a dragon all at the same time. "You are truly and luckily guided by the spirits of the old. You are just the person to help us find the princess." Jared did not know how to respond to that remark, so he just remained quiet.

Hurstle was not just the leader of his group but also the biggest, standing at least two heads taller than Jared. He had long shoulder-length brown hair and a long beard and mustache. His arms were about the thickness of Jared's head. And he wore a leather-studded vest. Jared thought he looked like a giant Viking. He even had a sword and several knives on him as well as a throwing axe.

Jonaria was the second in command. She was very muscular for a woman. But she was more like a gladiator than a woman anyway. She was the archer of the group. She could hit anything that she set her eyes on, moving or stationary—her accuracy was deadly. She had long golden hair, like the rest of the females in Onteria. But she was not the debutante of the ball. She had a unique beauty to her that Jared had rarely seen. She was confident and secure in her ability to protect anyone who needed to be protected.

Ferulous was a swordsman unmatched by anyone in the Kingdom of Onteria. His sword was brilliant-looking, adorned with jewels, gold, and silver. The sword matched its owner's looks. It was sleek and deadly, and that is how Ferulous looked. He was not big like Hurstle; he was more athletic and agile, allowing for quick movements. But like Hurstle, he also had long hair and a long beard.

Ferulous told Jared that he would be a fine addition to the three battle-hardened warriors' quest to find the princess since he had the Incognal spirit on his side. Being the impatient one out of the three, Ferulous also said, "It is time to go!" Hurstle agreed, and he told everyone to grab their gear. He then instructed Jonaria to lead the way.

Jared had now been away from home for over six hours, and Dave was getting anxious. He looked at Heather and said, "This is all because of that damn green stone he found."

Back at home, Heather got a concerned look on her face and asked, "What green stone?" She sounded alarmed. Dave told his wife the story Jared had shared with him about finding a green egg-shaped stone during the storm the other night. Heather was a little irritated that this was the first she was hearing about it. "Why didn't you tell me?" she asked in an exasperated voice.

"I didn't think it was that big a deal. I'm sorry."

Heather stood up and went to their bedroom to think. She was visibly upset, but Dave sensed it was more than just him not telling her about the Incognal. He went after her and asked her what was really wrong. By then, it was late in the afternoon. Heather sat silently for a couple of minutes. Then, she looked at Dave and asked him what the last thing Jared had said to him was.

Dave paused to try to remember. "Well, we had a little talk this morning, and Jared told me that the green egg thingy had magical powers and that it could transport him to another world. So, I told him to prove it to me. But when he held the egg, it didn't do anything, which made me mad because I felt like Jared was lying to me. I grounded him for not telling me the truth, and then, as I was leaving his room, he yelled out, 'I am telling the truth.' And that was the last time I heard from him."

Heather cried harder as though she knew something bad was going to happen to Jared. Dave asked her again what was really bothering her. He suspected that Heather knew more than she was letting on.

"I . . . I . . . just miss my son and want him back, is all," Heather said as she buried her face in the palms of her hands.

In Onteria, Jared and his new group were deep under the mountain. Hurstle told Jared, "These tunnels can go for hundreds of miles under the mountain before opening up to a common cavern." But he added that he didn't think that was the case with this tunnel. Hurstle knew because of the Incognal that they must be on the right path and that this particular tunnel would lead them to the princess. He was even more encouraged by the good fate of all four of them having chosen the same tunnel.

The Incognal vibrated and glowed brightly—so bright that everyone had to shade their eyes. They stopped and looked around, trying to figure out what the Incognal was alerting them to. Jared noticed that all around the walls of this section of the tunnel were markings that looked similar to the ones on the Incognal. Jonaria pointed out that since each Incognal has its own unique set of markings, the fact that the markings around them matched the Incognal must mean something significant. Ferulous suggested that maybe this was where the Incognal had been created. But no one knew for sure.

Along with the patterns on the walls, there were carvings depicting historical events. Jonaria explained that the carvings showed a war between tribes and the disappearance of a queen who was never seen again. But then, years later, a princess was born to a different tribe's queen. It was Princess Emera, and her mother—the queen—had died in childbirth, leaving Emera to fend off the other tribes fighting to take control of Onteria. The dominant tribe was led by Sadean, who had succeeded in poisoning Emera's mother during childbirth, causing it to look like she had died from childbirth. Sadean took Emera's father prisoner and kept him hidden from the world. Each event was intricately detailed in the carvings.

Jonaria noted, "It's been said that the Incognal only reveals itself to a pure-blooded heir to the throne of Onteria."

Jared laughed and told them he was born on Earth and had never been to Onteria before the other day when he met the princess. Hurstle suggested that maybe what they'd been told about the Incognal—the legends surrounding it—were wrong because obviously, Jared was not of their world. Jonaria agreed that not everything they'd been told could be true.

"Let's continue on our path," Hurstle commanded. The four of them remained mostly quiet for the next hour in the tunnel. But then, there was another vibration from the Incognal. Looking around, the group discovered a shaft that had been covered up by large stones. Ferulous kicked the stones, and the wall came crumbling down, opening up another tunnel. Without a word, they all knew they were to proceed down it.

As the group entered the new tunnel, it was lit up with the green glow of the Incognal. The tunnel's walls were scored with marks from weapons, indicating that a great battle had taken place there. "This must be where the tribe of the queen who disappeared battled another tribe," Hurstle posited.

The tunnel the group was in did not last long before it opened into an enormous cavern. The cavern was adorned with gold, silver, jewels, and crystals of all colors. It had been a magnificent banquet hall at one time. It was used to feed the people rebelling against Sadean. Hurstle, Jonaria, and Ferulous recognized the symbols that still covered the walls. They were symbols of Queen Meriza—the queen who led the rebellion against Sadean but then disappeared. The team of three kneeled in honor of the fallen, and Jared followed suit out of respect.

"Look!" Ferulous said, motioning to writing carved into the walls. "It's a warning. It says that only a pure-blood can choose the correct path out of this cavern. No magical being may assist, and the wrong path may lead to death."

Hurstle, Jonaria, and Ferulous all immediately turned to look at Jared. As the finder of an Incognal, he was the only one among them who was possibly of pure blood. There were many tunnels leading from the great hall. So, they had to choose the right one. Only one was the correct path, and the others were decoys filled with traps. Even the Incognal could not assist with the choice of tunnel since it was forbidden for any magical being to give aid. The choice was Jared's and Jared's alone. "Well?" Hurstle said, looking at Jared with questioning eyes.

Jared swallowed hard. He figured he would have to choose based on his gut feeling because that was all he really had to go off. There were over a dozen corridors they could take, and only one was the correct one. Jared figured they would know quickly whether they were on the correct path since the other ones would lead to their deaths. He was nervous.

Jared counted the corridors. There were thirteen of them. After a couple of minutes, he nodded toward one of the corridors and said, "Tunnel three." He paused for a moment, then said it again to be sure of himself. "Yes, it's tunnel three."

"Very well, then. Let's go," Hurstle said.

As soon as the group entered the tunnel, Jared had a sickening feeling that he had made the wrong choice. "This is the wrong tunnel! We need to get out of here!" Jared announced. The group immediately backed out of the tunnel. As they did, the ground in front of them crumbled and fell into a bottomless pit. Another step and they all would have perished.

Once they all were safe again, Jared took another guess. This time he said, "Tunnel seven." Jared took the lead and headed into the dark cavern. He felt more confident this time, and after they were all a few steps into the tunnel, the Incognal began glowing brightly, seemingly indicating that they were in the right passageway. A few more steps and a wall shot up behind them, closing them in. But they were still alive.

Jared led the way through the passage as the green glow of the Incognal lit the path forward. Along the way, they passed another wall with depictions of a battle. Jared was surprised that the queen who had disappeared—Queen Meriza—had been involved in so many battles in her fight against Sadean and other tribes trying to gain control of Onteria. All of the depictions they had encountered so far centered around her and her battles. Jared wondered where and how she had disappeared.

Chapter 5

Old Blood

A T ONE TIME, Sadean used an old Incognal that had been passed down to him from his father. But it eventually went dormant on him since he was nowhere near as pure as his father. His father was a nobleman who adored life in all manners and was a prominent supporter of Queen Meriza. That was before Sadean killed his father and created his own tribe and became a leader against Meriza.

Hurstle, Jonaria, Ferulous, and Jared were standing in front of the latest wall of carvings they had encountered. Jonaria pointed out that they were in an area that likely no one had been in for over one hundred years—ever since the queen vanished. The last pictures on the wall told the story of how Queen Meriza would return one day to defeat Sadean and his followers.

Jared noticed that there were some small inserts in the wall, just big enough to get one hand in. When he asked what they were, Hurstle explained that they were made for hiding clues for the next traveler who came by. Each member of the group reached a hand into an alcove to check for artifacts. The first go around, they all came up empty-handed. So, they each tried a different slot. They all came up empty-handed again, except for Jared. He pulled out a small dagger that was covered by a gold and green sheath with designs made of jewels.

Jared looked at the beautiful knife sheath, then pulled the knife out to get a good look at the blade. The designs on the blade reminded him of something. The motif on the blade and the hilt pattern were something that he had seen before, but he couldn't recall where. "I know this pattern," he informed the others. "It will come to me where I know it from . . . eventually."

The group checked each of the remaining alcoves, but the slots were all empty. Jared attached the knife to his belt, and they continued on their way down the tunnel. Eventually, the Incognal began vibrating harder than ever before. "Something is about to attack us," Jared warned the others. "I'm sure of it."

Hurstle, Jonaria, and Ferulous got in front of Jared, ready to defend the only possible pure-blooded one among them. And the muse around Jared's body tightened up around him. Even Olly, who had still been attached to Jared's leg this entire time, began growling and squeaking, ready to go to battle for him. The group sensed that something big was coming their way.

The Incognal's vibrations got stronger and stronger. Suddenly, a frightening beast appeared in front of the group. To Jared, it looked like a giant lion with the head of a dragon and the teeth of a saber-tooth tiger. It growled and snarled like it was preparing to attack, and it dug its front feet into the ground to get traction. The beast was so large that it barely fit in the tunnel.

The three battle-hardened individuals standing in front of Jared readied their weapons. They told Jared to get back as far as he could in case the beast got past them. Hurstle took the lead position with Ferulous next to him and Jonaria taking up the rear, ready to use her arrows and pinpoint accuracy. She would need it since the beast had skin as tough as iron, teeth as sharp as daggers, and razor-sharp claws. Jonaria knew that the beast's eyes would be its weak point, but she also figured that the beast could move extremely fast, making the eyes a tough target.

Suddenly, the beast charged. A furious war cry escaped Hurstle as he and Ferulous charged back toward the beast. Hurstle's knife throwing and Ferulous's sword swipes slowed the creature down, but the weapons bounced off its tough skin or were effortlessly batted away and down by its huge paws. Olly added to the efforts by jumping on the beast's back and digging his extremely sharp claws into the beast's neck. The giant cat-like animal made a full stop and tried to bat the tiny dragon off its neck. But Olly was too small and too fast for the enormous paws of the beast.

Hurstle yelled out for Jonaria to get ready. The beast let out a bloodcurdling growl, stomped its front paws, and charged again. Jonaria pulled back an arrow and let it go. The arrow soared past the two leading warriors and directly into the right eye of the beast. Though it did not kill the beast, it succeeded in slowing him down again.

The beast backed up and reared on its back legs as far as it could. It charged again. Another arrow flew past Hurstle and Ferulous. This time, Jonaria had pulled back as hard as she could. The arrow hit its target, penetrating the same eye and, this time, coming out the back of the skull of the beast's enormous head. The beast fell, and Jared took a deep breath as the three warriors in front of him put their weapons away. The monster was dead. Olly flew back to Jared's leg and began purring.

Ferulous walked up to the dead beast and swung his sword hard enough to break off one of the enormous teeth that hung eight inches down from the beast's mouth. He picked the tooth up and walked back to Jared, giving it to him. "Keep it as a sign of good luck and to use as a weapon," Ferulous instructed. "It also has healing properties."

Since the beast took up most of the tunnel, the group had to climb over the monster to continue on their way. The beast's skin was still as hard as iron as they crawled over it. Jared was speechless and still very intimidated by the beast.

Once the group got past the beast's body and continued on with the journey, Jared took up the number two position in line. He pulled out the tooth that Ferulous had given to him and noticed that it had what looked like gold and emerald inlaid in it. When he pointed it out to Hurstle, who was in the lead, Hurstle explained that it was indeed gold and emerald and that the marrow from the teeth has magical healing powers. "Don't lose it," he warned. "It could save someone's life."

Back in Jared's world, his parents, Dave and Heather, were in a panic. Jared had never been gone this long in his entire life. He had been gone all day, and it was now late at night. "What did the green egg look like?" Heather asked her husband.

Dave told Heather about the designs on the Incognal and

how the designs had circles and lines going through them. "For just a carved rock, it was heavier than I thought it would be," he noted.

Heather pulled out a piece of jewelry that Dave had never seen before and asked, "Were the designs like *this*?"

Dave's eyes got big. "Yes! They were. What do you know about the egg?" He could hardly believe what he was seeing as he looked at the piece of jewelry that had designs on it identical to the egg.

Heather took Dave by the hand and led him to the kitchen table, where they sat down. She started with, "I'm not who you think I am."

Dave got a confused look on his face, then said, "Go on."

"That green egg is not a rock; it's the spirit of my mother. It's called an Incognal."

"Yes, an Incognal! That's what Jared called it," Dave recalled. "What do you mean by the spirit of your mother, and what else do you know?" He was full of questions.

"I know that I'm not from this world—not from Earth. The world I'm from is called Onteria. My mother was the Queen of Onteria, but she was killed by an evil man named Sadean. He wanted her amulet—this one—for its pure power. So, I fled to *this* world to keep it safe from ever getting into his hands. If he ever got it, he could travel to any world and take it over, and nothing could stop him at that point."

Dave was in disbelief, but he told Heather he would keep an open mind about everything since she seemed to know a lot about what was going on. He was also quite upset that she had kept an enormous secret from him for so many years. He didn't know what to believe anymore. But right now was not about them; it was about how to get Jared back. "How did Jared get involved in all this?" Dave wanted to know.

"As my son and the grandson of the Queen of Onteria, Jared is the rightful heir to rule the Kingdom of Onteria. If Jared has been summoned by my mother in the form of the Incognal, then the current royalty in Onteria—Princess Emera—must be in trouble, and Jared is there to rescue her."

Heather paused for a moment to let Dave take everything in. Then, she continued. "After my mother died, I became the Queen of Onteria and ruled Onteria for hundreds of years. Then, tribal warfare for control of Onteria increased so much that I no longer felt I had the deference I needed to continue to rule. So, I went into hiding. When Princess Emera was born to the queen of another tribe, she became a beacon of hope for defeating Sadean's tribe and the other evil tribes. But if she is missing and Jared might be in trouble, it's clear I need to return to Onteria."

Dave still had doubts about whether what he was hearing was true. But he had always supported and believed in his wife. So, he said, "I'll go with you."

Heather smiled and said, "Let's get our son back." She had not been back to Onteria for one hundred years, so she was nervous. But she was still royalty—still the queen.

Dave followed Heather to their bedroom, where she pulled out an old box that he had never seen. She opened it, revealing a green amulet dangling from the end of a necklace. The amulet glowed as soon as Heather touched it. The box also contained a crown that was clearly meant for a great queen. "This crown belonged to my mother," Heather informed her husband.

Dave was speechless as his eyes surveyed the box's contents. He shook his head. "How do I know that everything you're telling me and I'm seeing is real and not just fairy tales?"

Heather took her husband by the hand and used her other hand to grab the glowing amulet that was now around her neck. Suddenly, Dave began to see an unfamiliar world come into focus, and he was speechless once more. Once Onteria had completely emerged in front of the couple, Heather looked at Dave and said, "Welcome to the world of Onteria." She set the crown on her head, and Dave noticed that her appearance had changed. Her hair glowed gold and shimmered with every move she made, and her eyes glistened like they were made from an ocean tide pool.

Onteria was not as beautiful as Heather remembered it. But that was because the princess was in trouble, and the colors in Onteria had responded. The sky was not its usual gorgeous color of purple with its orange sun. Instead, it had all gone dark. "Where are all the people?" Dave asked

"They have all gone into hiding until the princess returns or until . . . I retake my throne," Heather explained.

Dave felt guilty about the way he had treated Jared. He now knew that his son was telling the truth, and he decided the best way to make it up to Jared was by helping him rescue the princess. "You seem to have an extra glow about you," Dave said to Heather, shocked by her change in appearance.

"Oh, you haven't seen anything yet," Heather responded. She pulled her hair back, revealing pointy elf-like ears.

Dave stood with his mouth agape. "You're an *elf?*"

"Not just any elf. I am the *queen* of the elves. Now, let's get going. We have a long walk ahead of us." Heather knew the princess would not be in the palace. "If Sadean has Emera, she will likely be in the dark Caverns of Olna."

"Olna?"

"Yes, Olna. Olna was my mother's name. And the caverns are where her noble warriors went to seek guidance and prepare for battles. Many soldiers have been laid to rest in those caverns. But dark creatures lurk in the corridors now. It's the only place Sadean can rule until he gets the Amulet of Power."

"What is the Amulet of Power?"

"It's the jewel I have around my neck, and it's what's allowing you to see Onteria. I'm certain that Sadean planned the kidnapping of the princess to get me to show myself back in Onteria. He knew that as soon as the princess was in trouble, an Incognal would seek help from a pure blood or the queen and that I would bring the amulet with me. The Incognal that landed in our yard was likely intended for me, to get me to come out of hiding. But with Jared also being a pure blood, it attached itself to him when he found it first."

Dave's head was spinning. He felt like he was in an old fairy tale story book. His world had been turned upside down. In this new world, there were magic beings and amulets, fairies and elves, and colors he had never seen before. He was worried about what else might be waiting for them. But he was ready to help save his son.

Heather and Dave could see the palace on the horizon. But Heather pointed toward a large spire along a dark mountain range. "That's where we're going."

Dave's heart beat faster as he saw the ominous-looking spire marking the location of the dark Caverns of Olna. It scared him. He didn't know what to expect once they got there. But Heather told him that if he stayed close to her, he would be fine. She was a warrior queen who had fought in many battles. Dave still could not believe what he was hearing.

It was a long walk to the spire and the mountain range. Once the queen and Dave reached the spire, they noticed that the gates to the main tunnel were up. The queen told Dave that they only go up if there is an elf lord, like Sadean, that commands them to go up. "A trap has been set," she informed Dave. "It's likely that Jared took the bait and is inside, all alone."

What the queen and Dave didn't know is that at that moment, Jared's group had just past a dead beast and was headed down a tunnel that had smooth walls that lit up with color as they were touched. It had been a long journey so far, and they were all getting tired, so they stopped to rest. Ferulous told them he was not tired and that he would guard them all if they wanted to get some sleep. Jared was happy to hear that. He needed a break; it was the middle of the night for him back home.

The three of them—Jared, Hurstle, and Jonaria—lay on the ground, which was smooth like the walls. Hurstle and Jonaria were asleep in no time, but not Jared, who was nervous about an attack and couldn't sleep. Ferulous noticed he was awake, walked over to him, and assured him he would be safe in his guard. "Nothing will get past me," he said. That gesture made

Jared feel better. The floor was hard, but it had a warm sensation to it, and it hummed as Jared put his head on it. He finally relaxed and fell asleep within minutes.

Outside the main gate to the Caverns of Olna, the queen held up her amulet and commanded the gate to open, which it did, dropping back below ground. The queen and Dave entered the dark tunnel that led on for miles . . . *unless* you knew the shortcuts in the walls. The queen had been there many times, making plans with her soldiers. So, she knew all the shortcuts.

When the queen and Dave made it to the wall with the depictions of the battles on it, there was a hole in the wall that resembled the amulet the queen was wearing. The queen placed her amulet in the outline, and the wall opened to another tunnel. The tunnel would lead them straight to the grand banquet hall. They traversed it without any run-ins with dark entities or creatures.

When the queen and Dave arrived in the banquet hall, Dave was thunderstruck by the enormous cavern they stood in. He stood there, taking in the ornate hall that was adorned with ancient regalia. He had never been in a place this grand before, and he was at a loss for words to describe what he was seeing.

The queen told Dave to stick close to her when they entered the next corridor as she knew it was a dangerous one. Dave rushed to her side and said, "Oh, don't worry; I'm not leaving your side at all."

Being the queen and having been there countless times before, she knew the right tunnel to choose. As they entered the dark passageway where Jared's group had encountered the beast, Dave noted, "It sure is dark in here." The queen touched the amulet around her neck, and it lit up bright enough to dispel any shadows that might have been lurking. "Wow!" Dave exclaimed. "That will do!"

A little further down the tunnel, the queen came to an abrupt stop and ordered Dave to quickly get behind her. "I smell a beast," she informed him.

"Wh-wh-what kind of beast?" Dave stammered out.

"It's an enormous cat-like animal with the head of a dragon and teeth like a saber-tooth tiger," the queen explained. "Its paws are the size of basketballs, and it has razor-sharp claws that could penetrate these rock walls."

Just ahead of the queen and Dave, where the light was beginning to break away from the darkness, the beast that the three warriors had killed still lay there with a tooth missing. As the queen came upon it, she found the dead beast strange. Her son Jared could not have done this alone; he would not have known how to kill one of these creatures. Someone else was pursuing the princess, either with or without her son.

The queen and Dave crawled over the beast and continued on their journey. Dave followed his wife but could not believe what he had just done—the beast had been almost too big for them to crawl over. "I can't imagine how scared Jared must have been going up against that thing," he noted.

Up ahead, as Jared and two of his three companions were sleeping, Ferulous could hear voices coming from the tunnels behind them—the tunnels they had just come out of. But he did not alert the others. Instead, he positioned himself in the path so that he would encounter whoever—or whatever—it was first.

As the voices got louder, Ferulous raised his sword, ready to defend against dark creatures, dark entities, or anything else that might come around the corner. But when he saw a green glow coming up the tunnel, he knew that whatever was coming was friendly. Nevertheless, he held his sword ready, aware that not everything was always as it seemed in the Caverns of Olna.

When two people came around the corner, Ferulous stood his ground in their path. "Who are you?" the queen asked.

The battled-hardened warrior bellowed out, "I am Ferulous!" Ferulous's voice woke his three companions, who immediately jumped to their feet.

"Well, I am your queen. And I command you to let us pass!"

Jared, recognizing his mother's voice, called out, "Mom!" He ran toward her. Hurstle tried to stop him in case it was a trap, but Jared was too fast. Jared made it to his mother and wrapped his arms around her in an embrace.

As the queen came into sight of the others, Jonaria, being the oldest, remembered her. Jonaria's family had worked as guards for the queen before she disappeared. The two locked eyes, and the queen said, "It's good to see you again, Jonaria."

"It's good to see you again, too . . . Queen Meriza. Very good indeed!"

"Queen?!" Jared asked while staring at his mother with his mouth agape.

"We clearly have a lot to talk about, Jared," the queen responded.

Dave walked up to Jared, gave him a bear hug, and said, "I'm sorry for doubting you, son. I gave you such a hard time when I can see now that you were telling the truth."

"It's alright, Dad. You're here now, and that counts for a lot." Jared turned to look at his mom again. "Queen?! What have I missed?"

"After we find the princess and make it to the palace, I'll tell you everything," the queen assured her son.

"Yes, but . . . if you're the queen depicted on these walls, you must be several hundred years old. Can you at least explain how that's even possible?" Jared was glad to see his parents but extremely confused about the circumstances.

The queen provided Jared with the same information about her background that she had provided to her husband, then said, "I see you've made some new friends who are here to protect you."

Jared had gotten so used to the muse on his back and the rock dragon on his leg that he had forgotten they were even there. He explained that a mysterious man had appeared and given him the muse, and he asked his mother if she knew who it was.

"Yes, Jared. He is the caretaker of the royal muses and a dear friend of mine. This is an exquisite muse that has befriended you. It will now be your companion for your entire life."

"That little guy on your leg is very cute," Dave noted, motioning to the rock dragon. "Have you given him a name yet?"

"Yes. Olly is what I call him."

"Have you seen any tiny fairies flying around yet?" the queen asked.

"Not on this trip. But the first time I arrived in Onteria, I did. One landed on my shoulder and whispered in my ear."

"Do you remember what it told you? They are known for predicting the future."

"Yes. But it told me to keep it to myself."

Chapter 6

Reunion

QUEEN MERIZA LOOKED at the three warriors before her. Each of the warriors took a knee and vowed allegiance to their queen. She told them to rise and accept her gratitude for protecting her son, the heir to the throne of the Kingdom of Onteria. "The honor has been all ours, Your Majesty," Hurstle responded for the group. "Being in the presence of the old blood, in these chambers, on such an important quest has been a life-altering experience."

The queen looked at her son and told him, "I wish you would have come to me about the Incognal the morning after you found it. You and I used to tell each other everything, and I'm sad that we've gotten away from that."

"I didn't think anyone would believe me," Jared protested.

"You don't know until you try," Jared's mother reminded him.

"Yes, but I *did* try. I tried explaining it to dad and got grounded for not telling the truth."

Dave heard the comment and hung his head in shame for a

moment. Then, he lifted it, and with tears in his eyes, he said, "I was wrong, Jared. You should have been able to come to us about anything without fear of being believed."

"Well, no more secrets, then," Jared agreed. "I promise."

Hurstle interjected and said, "My Queen, we should get going. We have a long journey ahead of us." Queen Meriza agreed and told Hurstle to take the lead.

As the group was traveling through the long passageway, they came to a wall with depictions on it that Jared said looked like a family tree. The queen had hoped they wouldn't notice it and would just continue walking. There were secrets about their family that she wished they would not find out. Or at least, not find out *yet*.

At the end of a long line of royals listed on the wall was Meriza. Her mother was Olna, and her father was Gregor. And then Jared saw it. "You have a *brother*?!" The name had been partially scratched off, but Jared could still make it out. "*Sadean?!* This can't be true! He tried to kill me."

"The only reason he went after you was to try to lure me out of hiding. Now that I'm here, he has no real reason to harm you," Queen Meriza reassured her son.

"But how can someone so evil be your brother? What does he want."

"Ultimate ruling power. He wants this amulet around my neck, which would give him that power. He's always been jealous that the amulet went to me instead of him. Since he is my younger brother, he would never inherit the crown or power amulet unless everyone else in the line of succession was dead. And he seems determined to make that happen. He already killed our father, Gregor, who supported Queen Olna as the ruler of Onteria. Gregor was a commoner when Queen Olna married him, so he had no royal lineage."

As Queen Meriza was telling the story of her family, she became sad, and tears rolled down her face. She wiped them away and said, "Now you know the ugly truth. So, that's enough family history for today. Let's move on." Everyone had so many questions for the queen, but they kept them to themselves since they could see she was distressed.

The group continued walking. Suddenly, the amulet around the queen's neck flickered. She looked alarmed and told everyone to stop and take up a battle position. The muse screamed, and the little rock dragon squeaked. They were preparing for a fight!

Sadean appeared in the passageway and stood there ahead of the group, looking into Queen Meriza's eyes. "Hello, sister," he greeted her.

"You will never rule Onteria or any other world," the queen sternly replied without hesitation. "There's no way you can kill everyone in the line of succession."

"No? Well . . . I plan to try!" Sadean responded through gritted teeth.

The little rock dragon ran ten steps ahead of the group, toward Sadean, ready to attack. But Jared called him back. Olly looked disappointed but returned to Jared and wrapped around his leg and hissed.

Sadean brandished a great sword that had belonged to his father. It had been given to Gregor by his wife, Olna, on their wedding day, and it fell into Sadean's hands when he killed

Gregor. The sword was unbreakable, having been forged from star metal by a master blacksmith. "The only way to stop this is to kill me or to give me the Amulet of Power," Sadean asserted. "And I will not die easily!"

Like the crown and amulet, the sword was supposed to have been inherited by Queen Meriza. Having all three objects would make her even more powerful. She wanted what was rightly hers.

The three warriors prepare for battle against Sadean. He knew he could not beat them all at once. So, he lowered the great sword, and he said to the queen, "We will battle before this is over." Then, he disappeared back into the dark passageway behind him. Ferulous ran around the bend with his sword, ready to battle Sadean. But Sadean had already vanished.

"Sadean knows these tunnels as well as I do," Queen Meriza pointed out. "There are many hidden walls throughout these corridors. They can only be opened by either the amulet I wear or the ring he wears."

The queen got in front of everyone and told them she would take the lead because the next passageway could be daunting. She wanted Jared and Dave in the middle so that they would be protected. Then, she put her amulet against a wall, and a new passageway emerged in the ground. "It looks like we're going down," Dave noted. The path down was extremely dark. Not even the Incognal or amulet could produce enough light to guide them this time.

"We'll need to travel blind through this corridor," the queen warned everyone. When the rock dragon squawked, she said, "Oh, yes. Thank you for reminding me, Olly. The rock dragon can see in the dark. So, he can warn us of any danger. Stay close to the wall and use your hand to guide you to the end. Keep your hand on the wall at all times. *Never* remove it. Do you understand?"

Once everyone had confirmed that they understood the instructions, they proceeded into the dark cavern. The darkness quickly overtook their sense. Even the tiniest of light was swallowed up by the mysterious darkness of the corridor.

"I have a feeling we're being watched," Dave said.

"That's because we are," the queen confirmed. "This is the home of the rock dragons. They love the darkness, and this is where they hunt. They are all around us, watching."

"Will rock dragons a-a-attack humans?" Dave stammered out.

"Not unless they are provoked," the queen reassured her husband. "We are just passing by, so they shouldn't mind. This is the quickest way to the heart of the mountain, and we have no time to lose. So, just keep on walking, and keep your hand on the wall."

Everyone remained quiet. As they proceeded, they could hear the little patter of tiny dragon feet running all around. But everyone stayed calm.

When the group reached the end of the corridor, another passageway opened, and they reentered the light in a corridor filled with shimmering crystals on the walls. "After being in total darkness, it's stunning to have your first light be from crystals," Jared remarked. Everyone agreed that they were a beautiful sight to behold.

Chapter 7

Gain and Loss

THE QUEEN'S AMULET and Sadean's ring were made from special stones that came from the heavens. The stones were given to the siblings by Queen Olna on their eighteenth birthdays. But the young royals didn't begin to learn how to use them until they were close to twenty-two years old. They had to be trained by the master forger who had found the stones and created the jewelry.

The two pieces of stone were cut from the same rock. So, when the stones were close to one another, they would flash and become more powerful, sensing that they were close to being whole. But they had not been near each other for over one hundred years. Now that they were closer, both Queen Meriza and Sadean could feel the stones becoming more powerful. And when the jewels were at full power, they would give the wearer of both complete protection against harm. Queen Meriza had no doubt that Sadean's most recent appearance was to help him power his stone.

The rock from which the two pieces of stone were cut

came from the Caverns of Olna, deep in the heart of the mountains. The rock fell from the heavens while the mountain was being formed. The amulet the queen wore was the bigger of the two stones that had been cut from the rock. And if Sadean ever got a hold of both pieces, he would be unstoppable and could travel to other worlds and rule them all. That was the power of the stones once they were made whole.

Queen Meriza was certain she knew where Sadean was hiding. Her amulet was leading her to his location. She was also confident that she would find the princess there. Emera herself did not have any genuine power. She was merely a royalty figurehead until Queen Meriza returned from wherever she had disappeared to. Sadean had no real reason to harm Emera other than to try to lure his sister in so he could try to take the amulet.

Since the queen's stone was bigger, it held more power. So, she could navigate through the mountain quicker than Sadean. But at the end of the current corridor the group was traveling through, there stood a solid wall, blocking them from going any further. The queen did not remember this wall having ever been there before. It had no markings or indentations that the amulet could be placed in to open the wall. It was just a solid wall.

"Maybe we missed a turn somewhere back there," Dave suggested. But the queen knew there had been no turns they would have missed.

Hurstle, being the biggest person in the group, charged at the wall. As he hit the wall, it did not budge even the tiniest bit. The Queen said, "We cannot get through it. We need to go back." But as they all turned around to head back to where they had come from, the side walls began moving in on them. They were trapped. It was clear they could not get out of the tunnel before the walls closed all the way in on them.

The group ran through the dark tunnel, hoping there might be an offshoot they could enter, despite the queen's insistence that there wasn't. The walls had already closed so far in that everyone had to run in single file. The walls were not moving terribly fast, but the corridor was long, and the walls were steadily advancing inward.

A voice echoed through the cavern. It was Sadean, saying, "Give me the amulet, and you will all be saved! Don't, and you will all die, and I will get the stone anyway!"

The cavern was getting narrower. Ferulous turned his sword horizontal so that each end of it was touching a wall, hoping it might stop the walls from closing in. But the sword became embedded into the wall on both sides. Like the stones in the amulet and ring, his sword was made of star metal and was unbreakable. But the wall just closed in around it.

Panic was setting in among the group. They knew they would not make it out of the tunnel before the walls completely closed. By now, there were screams among them, and they turned their attention to fighting against the walls instead of running from them. Queen Meriza figured that, in her absence, Sadean's power over the Caverns of Olna must have grown stronger. She was shocked by how he could alter a passageway. *What does he know that I don't?* the queen wondered.

The walls were now so tight that everyone had to stand sideways and move sideways, especially the much larger warriors. Queen Meriza took her amulet in her hands and whispered words to it. The stone began glowing brighter and brighter. They all felt the mountain shake as the two great stones battled against each other for dominance. Even though the queen had the bigger stone, she had not used it for many years, giving Sadean plenty of time to learn more about the power of his own stone.

The walls finally started slowing down, almost to the point of stopping. But by now, no one had any room to move around. The amulet was glowing brighter than Queen Meriza had ever seen it glow. She could feel the power surging through her like she had never felt before. The walls were shaking, almost violently. The ceiling was crumbling down in some places, which created more problems for the group.

A piece of the ceiling fell and hit Jared in the head, knocking him out cold. But no one could get to him; there was no room to maneuver. Meriza saw what had happened to Jared, and she was overcome with emotions that gave her stone the power surge it needed to overpower Sadean's grip on the walls. The walls opened just enough for Dave to get to Jared and check on him.

Jared had a gash on his head and was bleeding badly. The muse wrapped tighter around him, fully enveloping him. Then, it let out a scream and changed its color to all yellow. Within minutes, the walls were more open, and Jared stood up. The muse had healed him. "They must have a very strong connection for the muse to be able to heal him that fast," Jonaria suggested.

"That was amazing!" Dave exclaimed. He was surprised

and overjoyed to see Jared recover so quickly.

The queen had never felt such power running through her before. She liked it. She learned that her emotions were connected to the amulet stone's power—something she never knew before. She knew that the wall blocking them at the end of the passage had never been there. So, she wanted to try her new knowledge of the amulet's powers on the wall.

Everyone turned around and headed back to the dead end. Once there, Queen Meriza put her hand on the wall while holding the amulet against it. She thought of something that would bring up raw emotions. She thought about when Sadean killed their father. And she thought about the subsequent years spent fighting for her kingdom and her life.

As the emotions welled up in the queen, the amulet shone brightly. It seemed to be as bright as a star, and everyone had to shield their eyes from it. The light concentrated on the rock wall, penetrating it and causing it to crumble down right in front of them. The passageway opened, and the group could continue on with its journey.

Hurstle took the lead this time. But as soon as he stepped over the crumbled wall, arrows began flying at the group. An arrow whizzed past Hurstle's head and embedded into Dave's chest. Everyone took cover behind the crumbled wall, where Dave had fallen.

Queen Meriza rushed to Dave's side and kneeled. "No!" she called out. When she saw where the arrow was embedded and Dave's condition, she was certain the arrow would kill him. It appeared to have penetrated both his heart and lung. And she could tell from the color of the arrow that it had been laced with poison.

Dave was having difficulty breathing, and his skin was turning a grayish blue from the poison. The whites of his eyes had filled up with blood from blood vessels bursting through-out his body. Jared kneeled on the other side of him and held hands with his father, though Dave's grip was weakening. Even Jared, who had never been involved in any kind of com-bat, could tell that his father was dying. Tears fell from Jared's face and landed on Dave's blood-soaked shirt.

Suddenly, Jared remembered the giant beast tooth Ferulous had given him and what Ferulous had said about it having healing powers. Jared removed the tooth from his pocket, but, not knowing how to use it, he looked to his mother for guid-ance. Meriza took the tooth, and Ferulous handed her a sharp knife. They knew she needed to get dust scrapings from the tooth into the hole in Dave's chest once they pulled the arrow out.

Dave screamed louder than he ever had before. Meriza knew that the pain he was about to feel was going to be excru-ciating. But it was necessary to save his life. Jonaria and Feru-lous took up positions on both sides of Dave, holding him down. Then, Hurstle grabbed the three-foot arrow sticking out of Dave's chest. With one solid pull from Hurstle, Dave screamed even louder. The Arrow was out of Dave's chest, but the dust needed to get into him quickly as he was fading fast.

The queen held the knife and the tooth over the hole in her husband's chest, which had air and blood bubbling up through it. She furiously scraped the tooth with the knife, quickly filling the bloody hole in Dave's chest with dust scrapings. The three warriors crowded around Dave were not convinced it would work since Dave was so far gone already. But they hoped it would.

Dave's chest began to steam and bubble as it appeared the hole was closing and cauterizing at the same time. But could the dust also stave off the poison? Jared was crying for his dad, begging him to stay alive. They had always been best friends, even during their recent turmoil over the Incognal.

The grayish-blue color of Dave's skin did not appear to be going away. When Jared saw that his mother was still worried, he was worried, too. The hole in Dave's chest was almost all the way closed, and the bleeding had stopped. But his eyes were now rolled back into his head. "Come back to us!" Jared yelled. "You can't leave!" Still holding Dave's hand, Jared could feel his father's skin go ice cold as the poison traveled through his body. By now, everyone was yelling for Dave to fight and open his eyes until he finally stopped breathing.

Tears streamed from Jared's face as he pulled his dad up into a hug. Jared looked up at his mom and noticed that she had tears falling from her face as well. "Can you save him?" he asked her.

"No, son. That is beyond my capabilities."

Jared rested his head on Dave's chest while Meriza put her hand on Jared's head. She wept more for Jared losing his father than for her losing a husband. And even Jonaria, who was usually stone-faced, shed a tear. She looked at her two hardened warrior companions, who were wiping away tears, too. "We must leave here," she said. "Otherwise, the shadow beasts will smell the dead body and be here in no time."

Meriza nodded her agreement and told Jared that they must leave Dave's body there. Jared's emotions were running high. He blurted out, "We can't leave him here to be eaten by shadow beasts." When Jared heard the words that were coming out of his mouth, they sounded ridiculous to him, given the normal and boring life he had been leading just a few days earlier.

"We must leave him, my son," the queen repeated. "Otherwise, when the poison starts seeping through his skin, it could contact you and kill you as well. Instead, it will kill the beasts."

Hurstle picked up Jared like he was no heavier than a paperweight and carried him away from his father's body. Jared wiped away his tears and said, "Sadean will die for this!" His mother had never seen Jared threaten anyone, so this was a new side of him. Though the circumstances seemed to warrant the way Jared felt, the queen hoped it would not taint her son's natural compassion toward others.

The group continued its journey but with one person less. They were all somber as they walked down the passageway. From behind them, they could hear the shadow beasts arriving at Dave's body and fighting over it. They were not worried about the shadow beasts following them because they were sure the poison would continue doing its job.

Jared never knew anyone who died before. It was a new experience for him, and he didn't know how to cope with it. His reaction was to want revenge. For the next hour, he was quiet. He would answer no one when they tried to talk to him. He was lost in his mind, plotting how he was going to kill Sadean.

Meriza knew what Jared was feeling and thinking because she had been there before when her own father was killed. All she could think of at that time was revenge—revenge against Sadean, her father's killer. The queen knew she needed to get through to Jared and get him out of the dark place he had been thrown into and back into the light.

The queen started with small talk, trying to get Jared's mind off his father. But all Jared said in response was, "We *are* going to kill Sadean, aren't we?"

The queen didn't know how to answer that question. She knew they needed to take Sadean's ring to strip him of his power, but she didn't want to teach her son that killing was the answer. "Maybe," was all she could reply.

Jared was annoyed with that answer, then angry. His anger burst out of him from every pore in his body. Meriza wished she could take away the pain he was experiencing, but she knew he had to work through it in his own way. She just hoped he wouldn't stay in the dark place he appeared to be in forever. She knew he needed to snap out of it, but she didn't know how he could do that when he was hurting as bad as he was. If Jared stayed in that dark place forever, he could end up just like Sadean, perpetually full of anger and the desire for revenge.

Chapter 8

Found

WHEN THE GROUP made it through and out of the last tunnel, they found themselves in the center of the mountain. Jared yelled out, "There she is!" Princess Emera was in chains at an altar, looking like she had been prepared to be sacrificed.

As Jared rushed over to the princess, his mother yelled, "Stop!" She knew it was a trap. But it was too late. Sadean came from around a corner and grabbed Jared.

Jared squirmed, trying to get away from Sadean. But Sadean was too strong—much stronger than Jared. Olly jumped off Jared's leg, jumped onto Jared's shoulder, and readied himself to attack Sadean. The tiny dragon was face-to-face with the attacker. He bared his teeth, ready to protect Jared.

Sadean held up his ring, and the jewel within it was glowing brightly. As Olly crouched down, ready to pounce on Sadean, the power of the ring's stone held Olly in place and kept him from attacking. When Sadean moved the ring, Olly was thrown off Jared's shoulder and onto the ground with one of his wings singed. "Leave him alone! Don't hurt him anymore!" Jared shouted. "Olly, come back to me!" Olly slowly wrapped himself around Jared's leg, tightened his grip as best he could, then turned and hissed at Sadean.

Sadean's next move was to use his ring to drop Jared's muse to the ground. Once Jared's backpack was exposed, Sadean ripped the pack off and threw that on the ground as well. Sadean gave the pack a good kick so that it and the Incognal were further away from Jared.

The warriors and the queen rushed toward Jared, ready to attack Sadean. But Sadean held a knife against Jared's throat, causing them to stop their advance. Jared tried to bargain with Sadean by offering himself, a pure-blooded heir, up for the princess. "I will voluntarily stay with you if the princess is released," he offered.

Queen Meriza immediately shouted, "No, Jared!" But Sadean had already taken him up on the offer. Since the princess was not part of their lineage, she was of less use to Sadean than Jared. Sadean dragged Jared to the altar and threw him down on the ground. The chains were removed from Emera and put on Jared. But Jared was not afraid; he had a plan.

There was still a connection between Jared and the Incognal. So, Jared concentrated as hard as he could on summoning the Incognal's power. He was so closely connected to it that he no longer needed to be touching it or even near it to use the power it possessed.

The princess ran to the queen. As she ran, Jared watched her with love-stricken eyes, making sure she was safe before he did anything. Princess Emera was exhausted from crying so much, but she always knew Jared would be the one to find her.

The Incognal glowed brightly from within the pack. Sadean noticed the pack glowing green and ran over to it. He removed the Incognal and tried to connect with it, but it was too late. Jared had full power over the Incognal. The chains that had been put around Jared melted away like they were made of butter. Sadean hadn't realized that Jared's connection to the Incognal had become that strong. Jared ran over to the warriors, who encircled him, protecting him from Sadean.

Sadean screamed his disapproval. He was angry that Jared had ruined his first attempt to get the amulet from the queen. But his attempts were not over yet. Now that Jared and the Incognal were so connected, Sadean knew that his only chance of getting the amulet was to remove Jared from the picture. Sadean disappeared down a dark corridor, leaving no trace.

The princess was extremely happy to have been rescued. The queen knew of a tunnel that would lead them right to the palace. She used her amulet to open the tunnel's entrance. They all had to be on the lookout for Sadean since he was still planning to get the amulet away from the queen. It was going to be a long and potentially dangerous trek back to the palace.

On their way back to the palace, the group encountered more pictographs of the queen's heritage. When they stopped at one chart, the queen put her amulet against the wall, and the wall came alive with depictions of the queen's mother and father. It brought a tear to her eyes while also making her mad as she remembered what her brother did to disgrace them by killing their father. She had never really felt that Sadean needed to die until now. Now, he had killed and tried to kill too many of her family members. Now, he must die.

The travelers made it back to the palace safely and without incident. But the queen knew that another attack was imminent, and the others felt the same. She was sure Sadean would bring reinforcements this time, too.

The palace walls held paintings of the queen's family going back thousands of years. Jared stood by one and asked, "Who is this?" As he looked at the painting, he felt like he was staring in a mirror, though the face staring back at him was much older.

The queen replied, "That is your great-grandfather. His name was Jarith."

There was a beacon that was to be lit as soon as the queen returned, so Princess Emera lit it. The entire Kingdom of Onteria would now know that its one true queen had returned. Within hours, the city and entire world of Onteria roared back to life with parties and bazaars and happy colors everywhere. Gifts and rare flowers were delivered to the palace for the queen and princess. Everyone in the entire kingdom seemed ecstatic to know that the princess was safe and that Queen Meriza had returned—everyone but Sadean and his followers, that is.

During the evening's festivities, the queen paused everyone for a moment of silence for her husband, Dave. Everyone stopped and mourned with her. Then, the parties resumed and continued throughout several subsequent days and nights. Jared had never seen such parties full of life and happiness before; colors were coming out of everything. But while everyone danced and partied, Sadean was planning his next attack with his followers.

The queen made Hurstle and his company of men the official guards of the royal family. And she appointed Ferulous as Jared's personal guard and protector. Jared was her son, the prince, and the next in line to rule Onteria. He must survive, no matter the cost.

Chapter 9

Fresh Start

ONCE ALL THE PARTYING in celebration of the queen's and princess's return had concluded, things in Onteria needed to get back to normal. The queen was back for the time being. But she still had a life and children in another world that she needed to get back to. Her daughters would be home soon from their camping trip, and she would need to tell them about their father, which she was not looking forward to.

Jared, however, planned to stay with Princess Emera in Onteria, he hoped forever. They wanted to get to know each other better. So, Emera agreed to take Jared on a tour of the entire city of Onteria as well as its outlying communities. Ferulous would, of course, be along for the tour as well.

Queen Meriza reacquainted herself with the city council members, some new and some old. They conferred and agreed that Sadean would not stop attacking cities until he got what he wanted: the Amulet of Power. The council assigned Hurstle and Jonaria to personally protect the queen from danger. The queen agreed, but she had already been back in Onteria for almost a full day cycle, and she informed the council that she could only stay for two more cycles before she needed to get back to her earthly home to collect her daughters and bring them to Onteria.

The queen still had her personal chambers that had been locked for all the years she had been gone. The chambers could only be opened by the amulet. There were other places in the palace that only the amulet would open as well. Meriza went to her room and placed the amulet against an indention next to the double doors, and both doors swung open for her. Her room lit up instantly, with light reflecting off crystals that covered the ceiling.

Meriza stood in the doorway to her chambers for a moment, soaking in the memories of a past life. Then, she walked into the room and shut the doors behind her. Off to the right was a sumptuous bed with ten-foot-tall pillars on all four corners. The bed was draped with the finest materials in Onteria and covered with a grand white spread that reached the floor. Countless pillows lined the edge of the bed against the wall. The headboard was ornate with designs of swirls and circles that represented all the other worlds around Onteria. And the headboard contained a slot for the queen's amulet to sit in. When the queen placed the amulet in the slot, the headboard's engravings lit up.

Next to the bed was a desk that had been made from the extinct wood of plantera. The desk was a gift from the queen's father, Gregor, a skilled woodworker. The room's walls were covered with stone mined from the heart of Olna Mountain. The stone walls adapted their colors to the queen's mood. They were currently all a bluish-red color you might even call a shade of purple. This meant that the queen was both happy and sad at the same time. She mourned the loss of Dave, missing him immensely. But she took comfort that her children would be a reminder of him that she would cherish.

The rest of the queen's room was mostly comprised of closets and dressers full of clothes as well as items given to her from figureheads of other cities across the Kingdom of Onteria. When a figurehead visited the queen, they would stay in the palace as a guest, and it was customary for them to bring a gift to give to the queen. Treasures lined her walls, and she loved them all.

There was, however, one gift that the queen treasured above all others. It was a piece of glass made from lightning. The queen and her brother, Sadean, found the glass in the crystal sands of a beach when they were kids. Meriza loved Sadean very much at that time, before he began to change. But as he grew older and realized that he was not in line to be the ruler of Onteria, he wanted more power. Meriza missed the innocent times spent with her brother as a child, but they were just memories now. Now, Sadean wanted her and the rest of the family line dead.

Queen Meriza sat down on the edge of her bed and cried. She had lost her husband and her brother. She suddenly felt very alone. She hoped that Jared, being next in line to rule after her, did not possess any of Sadean's jealous or evil intentions.

Jared was, at that moment, enjoying a tour of the city of Onteria and meeting its residents with Princess Emera. It was much more immense than the cities he was used to back home.

He figured that Onteria must be three times the size of Denver, Colorado. With such a large city, Emera had planned for a multiday tour. There was far too much to see and experience in just one day!

As for Sadean, he was in his hideout in Dark Mountain, which was over 100 miles outside the city, beyond Olna Mountain. There were tunnels leading from Olna Mountain to Dark Mountain, which is how he got there after vanishing from the cavern at the heart of Olna Mountain. After Queen Meriza vanished from Onteria, Sadean spent many years developing the tunnel system and his hideout in preparation for her return. Meriza did not know the new tunnels or hideout existed.

Within Dark Mountain, Sadean had many followers awaiting his command. With their original plan for luring in the queen having gone awry, they now planned to attack the city of Onteria and the palace directly. Their specific targets were the pure bloods Jared and Queen Meriza and, to that end, also Princess Emera. They would kill whoever they needed to in order to obtain the amulet and rule Onteria and all worlds beyond it.

One of Sadean's followers reported back to him that Jared and the princess were on a tour of the kingdom and that they only had one guard to protect them. Sadean knew that the first step of his plan had to be to kill Ferulous. But he was not aware of all Ferulous was capable of. Ferulous was the most skilled swordsman the kingdom had ever seen. He had been trained by the best swordsman, and that swordsman had also been trained by the best. The sword that Ferulous carried had been passed down from master to apprentice for over 1,000 years. It was made of star metal and was unbreakable.

Sadean's attack was to begin in two days, and Sadean had well over 600 followers ready to fight on his behalf. Queen Meriza had an army of Onterians that was well over 10,000 strong, and they were all battle-hardened soldiers. Figuring that it would not be long before Sadean tried something, the queen planned to meet with the commanders of her army to put them on alert. She wanted to stay to oversee things in the event of an attack but also knew that she needed to return to the Earth world to collect her daughters. She was torn on what to do.

After thinking it over for some time, the queen decided to give Princess Emera and Jared the duty of meeting with the commanders of the army to let them know of a possible attack from Sadean on the city and its people. With Emera already having leadership experience from having served in the queen's stead and with Jared next in line after the queen to take the throne, she figured it was appropriate for them to take the lead on preparing the army and the city for battle.

Jared still had his companion, Olly. And Olly was friendly with most of the people they met on their tour of the city. Rock dragons truly were loyal and protective once they found the right companion. It differed from the muse protecting Jared, which was dependable but still very much a wild creature. The muse circled Jared from above, watching him and making sure he was not in danger. The Incognal was at the palace, safe in a vault with all the other valuable relics the kingdom had discovered over the years.

Having received the queen's instructions, Jared and the princess paused their tour to meet with the commanders of

Onteria's army. There were five commanders—one for each battalion. The commanders, in turn, put the entire army on high alert to be prepared for Sadean and his followers. But, unbeknownst to them, one of the commanders was a follower of Sadean and alerted him to key defensive plans and positions.

Jared and Emera, figuring it was now too dangerous to continue their tour of the city, began making their way back to the palace. But suddenly, they witnessed a huge explosion at the entrance of a bazaar. This was simply a test from Sadean to see how Ferulous would react in protecting Jared and Emera. Sadean was disappointed that Ferulous immediately went toward them, protecting them, instead of away from them. In fact, Ferulous ushered the two of them straight back to the palace even faster than before.

At the palace, the queen was getting ready to head back to her home on Earth so she could get her daughters. She could still come and go from Onteria as she pleased with the power of the amulet. Having received word of the blast, the queen decided to have Hurstle accompany her wherever she went until she left Onteria. He could not go with her to the Earth world, though. With his enormous size and appearance, not to mention his knives and sword, he would stick out there like a sore thumb.

When the time had come, the queen used her amulet to exit Onteria and reenter the Earth world. She was transported back to the exact spot she had been in when she left the Earth world—her bedroom at home. She arrived there before the twins returned from their camping trip, and being alone in the house made her feel sad. It seemed that everywhere she looked, there was a reminder of Dave, including a framed wedding photo on their bedroom wall.

Heather, as she was known in the Earth world, heard the sound of a key turning in the lock of the front door. The girls were home. They came bounding in the door as noisy as usual. They had clearly had a great time, and hearing their excitement and laughter brought a quick moment of joy to Heather. She burst into tears from both sadness and happiness. The girls dropped their gear on the living room floor and went looking for their parents.

When Anna and Stephany found their mother at the kitchen table, Stephany immediately asked, "Where is Dad?" He was not in his usual chair across from Heather, where he always sat so he could look directly into her eyes. Then, the twins noticed their mother was crying. "Are you okay, Mom?" Stephany asked.

"No. No, I'm not okay. We need to talk. But please just give me a minute." After several minutes of the twins watching Heather breakdown, she finally regained her composure and was ready to talk. "Please take a seat, girls," she insisted. The girls both sat down across from her. She took their hands, one hand in each of hers.

"What's going on, Mom?" Anna asked. "You're scaring us."

Heather didn't know any other way than to come out and say it. "Your father is dead. When we went to try to find Jared, there was an . . . accident."

The girls gasped at the same time. "Was it in the . . . *other* world?" Stephany asked.

"Quiet, you dolt," Anna scolded.

"It's okay," Heather insisted. "I know you both know about the other world. Jared told me you do. And yes, it was in the other world."

It took the girls several minutes to begin trying to process what they had just been told. After what seemed like a long silence, they both broke down into tears—one after the other. Heather stood up, went around the table, and hugged both twins at once. But it was of little comfort to them. They were heartbroken to have lost their father.

After an hour had gone by and the tears began to dry up for the time being, Heather decided to tell the twins as much of the rest of the story as she thought they could handle. "What you need to know is that I know about that other world because I am . . . *from* that world."

The girls knew their mother was serious because no one would make a joke at a time like this. Anna began rattling off questions. "How is that possible? Why are you here? How long have you been here? Where did—"

"Slow down!" Heather pleaded. "Just slow down, girls. I will explain everything." She started at the beginning, with why she left her world and came to Earth, to hide from her evil brother. And she ended with the most recent event, the explosion in the bazaar. The entire story took well over an hour to tell, especially with all the questions Heather had to answer along the way. Although the girls looked shocked and confused, Heather could sense that they understood and believed her.

"Wait! If you are a queen, doesn't that mean that Stephany

and I are . . . *princesses*?" Anna asked with excitement.

"Yes, that's true," Heather confirmed. "And Jared is a prince." Anna scoffed at the thought of it. "As the oldest, he is also the next in line to rule after me."

"Can we *go* to Onteria?" Stephany asked.

"Yes. In fact, with your father gone, with Jared in Onteria, and with the people of Onteria needing me more than ever, I have no choice but to bring you there now. We don't have much time, though. Gather only your most important necessities, and then we'll go. There's a guard waiting there for our return." The girls were still full of questions, but all Heather would say in response was, "You'll see when we get there."

When the queen and her girls arrived in Onteria, Hurstle was still right where she left him, waiting. *He is a darn good soldier*, the queen thought. As always, the queen had returned to the exact spot she last exited from: this time, her palace chambers. There, she took a long look out a window and was happy to see that the city and the palace were still intact.

The girls took a long look out the windows as well, and they were amazed by what they were seeing. It was like a fairy tale that had come to life. As Stephany looked out a window, a tiny fairy flew in, landed on her shoulder, and whispered in her ear. She suddenly got a huge smile on her face. "What is it? What did it say?" Anna wanted to know. But Stephany knew that she had to keep the fairy's message a secret. Anna was jealous.

Jared was thrilled to see his sisters—even Anna. He ran up to them and hugged them both around the neck at one time. Then, at their mother's insistence, he showed the girls around the palace, introduced them to the guards, and took them to their rooms. The girls' rooms were identical and were opulently set up for princesses. The forward-facing walls had shelves full of ornate tiaras for all occasions. The back of the rooms were full of handcrafted gowns. And the designer beds sat on floors of color-changing marble. Crystals covered the ceilings. The twins were speechless as they took it all in for several minutes.

"Thank you for the tour, Jared," Stephany finally said. "The palace and these rooms are beautiful." Stephany's tone was somber as she spoke. She was sad for all of them that they had lost their father. She gave Jared a long, tight hug. When Olly chirped at her, she said, "Bye, Olly." Then, she vanished into her room, shutting the doors behind her.

Jared found his mother in the palace's dining room, sitting at an enormously long table, looking distraught. "We've received a message from Sadean," she informed Jared. "He says we have until midnight to hand over the kingdom to him, or he and his followers will begin their attack."

"What are you going to do?" Jared asked.

"Fight to the end!" the queen asserted.

Jared smiled. "To Dad, then!"

"To Dad!" the queen replied.

Jonaria was given a new assignment. She was to guard the twins from harm. But since Sadean didn't know the twins were in Onteria, she figured that they were less likely to be harmed than Jared or Queen Meriza. The twins mostly stayed in their rooms, high up in the palace, throughout the day. And everyone was okay with that.

Sadean had spies watching Jared's every move. He was dismayed when they reported back that Ferulous never left Jared's side, which was going to be a problem for Sadean. Princess Emera was also often at Jared's side as the two spent as much time getting to know each other as possible. Jared was captivated by Emera, and he was falling in love, even though they had only recently met.

Since Sadean was not planning to attack until after midnight, Jared and Princess Emera decided to take a final walk outside the palace before things turned for the worse. It was just the two of them but with Olly wrapped around Jared's leg and Ferulous following a few yards behind to give them privacy but keep them safe. Ferulous never took his eyes off the two of them.

Suddenly, something felt off to Ferulous. "Stop!" he called out to Jared and the princess. "Get down!" Jared and Emera did what they were told, taking cover behind a nearby cart. Ferulous heard arrows whizzing through the air. He began to yell for more guards to come help secure the two prized targets, but before he could finish speaking, he was struck in the chest with an arrow. The wound was not life-threatening but had penetrated enough of Ferulous's right lung that he could not get enough breath to continue yelling.

More arrows went flying. Ferulous took out his sword, and with fast strikes, he batted the arrows away from him while yelling in pain from the arrow stuck in his chest. While he was preoccupied with the arrows, men in dark cloaks came running out from the darkness. They grabbed Jared and the princess despite Jared fighting the men as hard as he could and yelling for Ferulous to help. Ferulous pulled out a throwing knife and launched it. The knife pierced the neck of the assailant who had hold of the princess. The assailant dropped to the ground, and the princess was free. "Run, Emera!" Jared called out.

Several palace guards heard all the yelling and commotion and arrived at the scene. But by then, Jared was gone and Ferulous had two arrows in him. Only the princess had been saved unscathed. The guards quickly made Queen Meriza aware of the attack and Jared's abduction.

The queen was furious that Jared and the princess had been allowed to leave the safety of the palace walls during a period of high alert and that Sadean's men could so easily sneak onto the palace grounds. And she was sad about the injuries sustained by Ferulous, who was in the palace infirmary. There, the doctors had already removed one arrow, but the one in Ferulous's lung remained. The queen appeared in the infirmary and asked Ferulous, "What happened down there?"

"It was an ambush, Your Highness. They were hiding in the darkness."

"Where were all the other guards?" the queen demanded to know. "Were they not at their posts?"

"No, they weren't. They were relieved by the captain of the guards. There were almost no guards around. I figured they had been positioned elsewhere, in preparation for the impending battle."

"Go find the captain, Hurstle!" the queen ordered. Hurstle was reluctant to leave the queen's side during such a dangerous time, but he figured that detaining the captain was the way in which he could most help keep her and everyone else safe at the present time. As he was exiting the infirmary, the queen called after him, "And tell the other commanders to make sure there are guards on all posts around the palace."

"Yes, Your Highness," Ferulous agreed. "I will handle it." And with that, he was off on his mission.

The queen went to her library to think. After a few minutes, Stephany walked in and asked, "What's wrong now, Mom?"

"Your brother has been taken," the queen replied.

"Oh, no! Are we going to be able to find him? What are they going to do with him until we do? What can we do?" Stephany was clearly panicked.

"Take a deep breath, honey. We'll get him back. I assure you."

Then, Princess Emera entered the library and sat next to the queen. "This was all my fault, Your Majesty. I'm sorry. I was the one who wanted to go walking outside one last time before the battle began."

"No, it isn't," the queen insisted. "No one could have known that one of our commanders has been turned. A lot has changed since I left for the Earth world over one hundred years ago. Loyalties have shifted. I'm just glad they didn't abduct you as well."

"I believe I know where Sadean is," Emera announced. "While you were in hiding in the Earth world, there were reports that Sadean had been building an army in a hideout in Dark Mountain."

"Then, we must go there!" Stephany called out.

"No! My queen must not go there," Hurstle protested as he

walked into the room. "It's too dangerous to send a pure blood with so few of you left. My team and I, including Jonaria and Ferulous, will go get Sadean."

"Ferulous can't go with you; he's injured," Queen Meriza pointed out.

"He's been injured before, and much worse than this time. He is built like a gladiator and will be fine. In fact, he's already in the armory preparing for the rescue."

Ferulous and Jonaria were indeed in the armory, loading up on weapons. "How goes it?" Hurstle asked when he walked in. He was glad to have the trio of warriors back together, even with the daunting circumstances behind the reunion.

"We'll be ready shortly, Hurstle," Jonaria responded. "But where exactly are we going?"

"Dark Mountain. We leave at midnight, under the cover of darkness. There is no moon tonight."

The warriors finished gathering the additional weapons they needed for their assault. Then, the three of them reported to the queen just before they planned to head out. "Be safe, my warriors," she said. "And bring back my son."

"We will, My Queen," Hurstle assured her. But what of Sadean?"

The queen did not hesitate in responding, "*Kill* him." She couldn't believe those words had come out of her mouth. But Sadean had gone too far and would only get worse if he wasn't completely stopped.

It was midnight, and the trio of warriors was off on their mission. It was only the three of them, but they were the best hope Jared had of coming back alive. It was a perfect night with a cool breeze and no moon. To reach Dark Mountain, they had to walk around Olna Mountain. It was going to be a long trek, but they would reach Dark Mountain by sunrise. Hurstle liked it best when they traveled in the dark, and it could not get any darker that night.

The queen and the twins were in her room, sitting on the bed. They were scared for Jared, not knowing if he would come out of this alive. The girls could not bear to lose anyone else. They wanted their brother back safe. "Hurstle and his team are the best," the queen reassured her girls. "They will bring him back. Now, go to bed and sleep." The twins went to their rooms and went to bed. But the queen sat up all night, hoping for news about the rescue mission.

Ferulous was still pained from his injuries, but he only slowed the group down a little. He felt foolish that Jared had been taken under his watch, and he was determined to redeem himself by rescuing the queen's son. He was fueled with anger and wanted blood. The captain of the guard had set him up. "The captain is mine to kill," he told the other two warriors. They nodded their agreement.

By the time the warriors had been traveling for four hours, they were getting close to Dark Mountain. But Dark Mountain sat within a vast mountain range. The warriors still had at least two hours to go before they would reach the Dark Mountain's caverns.

Chapter 10

Dark Mountain

THE THREE-PERSON TEAM of warriors was ready to fight. They now had just one hour to go before they reached Dark Mountain's caverns. The terrain was rough, with no smooth footings. And all around the warriors were thorny vines that burned when they touched the warriors' skin. The rocks around them were jagged and as sharp as blades. But the warriors persevered. They would get Jared back.

The early morning sky was full of stars that were brilliantly lit to guide the way. The morning air was still cool with a little briskness to it, but the warriors were prepared for that. And the cool air kept them from overheating. Their arms were covered with blood spots from the thorny vines that they trekked through, but that was the least of Ferulous's worries.

Hurstle was dressed in loose pants and a leather vest. His boots were calf-high and were covered in thorns that had broken off on the leather sides. He had a sword and knives dangling from his waist.

Ferulous was in the same type of pants and boots as

Hurstle, but he was wrapped in a bandage where the arrows had struck him. He had a leather vest as well, but his was covered with an ornate circle of armor in the front and back. He even had shoulder leathers. His attire was appropriate for sword or knife fighting.

Jonaria wore short pants that went to her knees and a loose-fitting top. She needed to be agile to pull back an arrow as fast as she could time and time again. She had the most blood spots on her arms and legs, but she was not one to complain.

The three warriors were each ready for battle in their own way, but they had a common goal: to rescue Jared. Rescuing a pure blood and saving the kingdom from the evil Sadean was a noble cause. The warriors wouldn't think twice about killing anyone who stood in their way.

Back at the palace, Queen Meriza was still up and pacing in her room. At that point, there was little she could do to help get Jared back. The only thing she could do would be to voluntarily give up her amulet to Sadean. She felt that her son's life was more important to her than ruling Onteria or keeping the powerful amulet. So, after a lot of thought, she decided to give into Sadean's demands rather than lose her only son. The queen used a secret passageway to escape her room without the palace guards noticing. Once outside the palace, she stole extra guard equipment to wear and went to the animal stalls to get what resembled a horse. But this animal was larger than any horse and faster. Queen Meriza was ready to go.

At Dark Mountain, Jared was being kept in a large, open fissure in the center of the mountain. His hands and legs were tied. And he had been beaten repeatedly by the captain of the guard. Jared was bloodied, and his clothes were torn. But any time he was asked to do something, he continued to refuse.

Jared's muse, thinking Jared was safe under the watchful eye of Ferulous, had flown off during Jared and Emera's walk. And the captain had kicked Olly off Jared's leg as soon as they left the palace grounds. But rock dragons could see in the dark and were excellent trackers. Olly eventually caught up and saw Jared tied up just as the captain was kicking Jared in the side. The loyal rock dragons were also excellent hunters and protectors. If you hurt one's person, they would become barbarous and make you pay for it. Immediately after the captain kicked Jared, Olly attacked with his sharp teeth, powerful jaw, and long, retractable claws. He locked onto the captain's upper thigh and was tearing into him.

Despite being turned in the opposite direction, Jared could hear the growling, screaming, and commotion and knew what was happening. As Olly and the captain tumbled into view, Jared could see his rock dragon attached to the captain's leg and continuing to tear into it. Blood and skin were flying everywhere. Eventually, Olly had bitten and clawed so deeply that the captain's artery was severed. The captain tumbled to the ground, holding what was left of his leg as blood drained from it. Within minutes, he had perished.

Olly scurried over to his person and bit Jared's restraints off in a mere three bites. The leather straps were no match for Olly's razor-sharp teeth. Then, Olly squealed and bounced up and down as Jared told him he was a good boy. Olly lovingly reattached himself to Jared's leg and began purring. Jared grabbed a knife off the captain's belt and headed toward the fissure's one exit, which led to a tunnel. But it was no use. As Jared and Olly entered the tunnel, they were met by what seemed like an army of guards that immediately took Jared back into custody. "Sadean would like to have a word with you," one of the guards growled out.

"Olly, run and hide!" Jared shouted as the guards began dragging him away down the tunnel. The rock dragon jumped off Jared's leg and disappeared into a pile of dark rocks. As the guards dragged Jared through a maze of tunnels and caverns, Olly followed closely behind, unseen and unheard. Jared and the guards were headed to the heart of the mountain, where Sadean and his army of followers awaited them. Sadean's lair, a large opening in the center of Dark Mountain, was full of color crystals and naturally changing stone floor that changed with every step someone took. If it were not a prison for Jared, he would have found the chamber quite beautiful.

Hurstle and his team were now also in Dark Mountain's caverns. They had never been there before but knew that most mountains in Onteria had hollowed-out chambers toward the middle. So, that is where they headed. The queen was headed there as well, having just passed Olna Mountain. Her trusty horse-like animal was quick. With every powerful stride, she could feel its muscles bulge from its sides and down its legs. It was an impressive animal.

Back at the palace, the twins woke up and discovered that their mother was not there. Nobody was certain where she had gone, but the palace guards told the girls that they suspected she had gone to Dark Mountain to help save Jared. The twins were fearful for her and Jared's lives. If the twins lost both of their remaining family members, they didn't know what they would do. And the girls were sure that when Sadean discovered their existence, they would be next on his kill list as the remaining heirs to the throne. For the time being, at least a dozen guards escorted the girls to an elaborate breakfast spread. Everyone hoped it would help keep the sisters somewhat distracted.

Jared now found himself face-to-face with Sadean. Sadean struck Jared in the face, leaving a red handprint on his cheek. "You are more trouble than you are worth!" Sadean shouted. "No matter, you will die soon."

Jared noticed that the ring Sadean was wearing was glowing. He remembered what his mother had told him about the ring. When her amulet and the ring get close, they glow. Jared knew that at that moment, there was a rescue attempt underway. Indeed, the queen was now at the mouth of the entrance to Dark Mountain, not far behind Hurstle and his team. It would be easy for the queen to find Sadean with her amulet guiding the way.

Dark Mountain was full of color crystals, but some of them were dark crystals, which could drain your life essence away and kill you. The crystals are how Dark Mountain got its name. Although the queen had her amulet to protect and guide her, and Sadean had his ring to protect and guide him, the three warriors took a wrong turn and ended up in a cavity filled with dark crystals. They immediately felt the effects of the crystals. The warriors were losing energy fast, but they didn't know which way to turn next.

Suddenly, the warriors heard a squeal. When they looked

toward the direction the squeal came from, there was Olly. He was bouncing around like he wanted them to follow him. "By all means, lead the way, Olly!" Ferulous insisted. Olly first led them to the third opening on the left, into a cavern filled with color crystals that would restore the warriors' energy. "Thank you, Olly, but where is Jared?" Ferulous asked.

Olly squawked and ran down another tunnel. The warriors ran after him. "Good boy, Olly!" Jonaria called out as the rock dragon bounded from rock to rock ahead of the trio.

The queen was rushing down a tunnel when she heard footsteps coming toward her. She froze. There was no place to hide. Meriza pulled her sword and prepared to stand her ground. The footsteps were now just seconds away. The queen's heart was beating faster, but she was ready to defend herself. Just as she went to strike her sword at who ever came around the bend in the tunnel, out popped little Olly. Then, Hurstle and his team followed.

"My Queen!" Hurstle exclaimed with surprise. "What are *you* doing here? This is no place for you."

"I'm here to save my son," the queen sternly replied. "I'll give Sadean my amulet in exchange for Jared's life."

"You can't do that!" Jonaria shouted. "There is more at stake than just one life. Once Sadean has both the amulet and ring, he will be able to rule all worlds, not just Onteria. You and your family will never be safe from him. Nobody will be."

"But if I don't do it, Jared will likely die. And I've lost too much already. This is my decision, and as your queen, I expect you to honor it."

"We will, My Queen," Ferulous agreed. "But let us try

first. We saved Jared once; we can do it again. If we don't, then you can offer an exchange. But . . . let us try."

"Okay, we'll try your way first," Meriza reluctantly agreed. "But if it looks like Jared's life is in danger, I will step in and make my offer."

"Yes, My Queen," Hurstle answered for the trio of warriors.

Sadean's ring continued to glow brighter and brighter. But nobody other than Jared seemed to notice, including Sadean, who was intently focused on Jared. Jared looked toward the only tunnel leading into Sadean's lair, hoping a team of rescuers would burst through it. Instead, he noticed Olly perched high on a rock, crouched down like he was hunting prey. Then, from out of the darkness of the tunnel, a knife came flying through the air toward Sadean. At the same time, Hurstle appeared in the tunnel's opening.

Sadean dodged the knife, which ended up embedded in one of his guards. He then ordered his remaining army of guards into action. The guards rushed toward Hurstle, pushing him and the other warriors back into the tunnel from whence they had come. Amid the chaos, Sadean still had not noticed his ring glowing.

The warriors, anticipating that Sadean and his followers would overwhelm them once they reached Sadean's lair, had hidden the queen in an offshoot of the tunnel. Queen Meriza held her amulet in her hand and concentrated on the amulet and its power. She visualized swirling rings of energy spinning around her. She could feel the power of the amulet welling up inside of her. The amulet changed from a blue color to a fiery red. As Sadean came by her hiding spot in the tunnel, the queen reached the amulet out to touch Sadean and shock him. But when she was just inches away from him, a guard grabbed her arm. The guard yelled in pain and fell away as he absorbed the shock that had been intended for Sadean. Sadean turned his head, and the estranged brother and sister locked eyes.

The queen had used up the swirling power on the guard, so the amulet returned to a blue color. Sadean grabbed the queen, ripped her from her hiding spot, and held her around the neck between himself and the warriors, using her as a shield. But Hurstle instinctively grabbed one of his throwing knives, and with one quick snap of his wrist, he sent the knife spinning toward Sadean's head. With the ring and the amulet so close together, there was a power field around Sadean and the queen, protecting them. The knife bounced off Sadean and fell to the ground.

Sadean ordered the warriors to back up and drop their weapons or he would cut the queen's throat. They now had no choice but to do what he told them. Once their weapons were laid down, Sadean ordered his guards to push the warriors further back in the tunnel until they were back in the cavern of dark crystals. There, the warriors fell to the ground as their energy began to drain quickly.

Jared was dismayed to see Sadean reenter his lair with the queen in his grasp. Once they were in the large hollow, Sadean threw her to the floor next to Jared. When Jared leaned down over his mother to check her wellbeing, Sadean reached down to pluck him off the ground. But before Sadean had the chance to do so, Olly jumped on him. As Olly tried to sink his teeth and nails into Sadean, he discovered he was unable to do so due to the power shield of the ring and amulet being so close together. But Olly created enough of a distraction that Jared was able to take hold of Sadean's hand and rip the ring from it.

Jared tossed the ring as far as he could into the rocks from which Olly had just come so that it would be as far away from the amulet as possible. Olly tried sinking his teeth and claws into Sadean again, and this time, he succeeded. As Sadean held his injured and bleeding arm, he ran out through the tunnel and disappeared into the darkness. It was only then that he calmed down enough to realize that his ring was gone. He stood there looking at the empty hand where his ring used to be and at his injured arm and let out a blood-curdling scream. He wanted to go back to retrieve the ring, but with his arm spewing blood and with his guards tied up by the warriors, he knew he couldn't.

Jared quickly located the ring and brought it over to his mother so that the ring and the amulet were close together. "Sadean's men can't harm us now," the queen excitedly said. "We need to get Hurstle, Ferulous, and Jonaria away from the dark crystals before they die!"

Queen Meriza and Jared rushed through the tunnel, back to the dark crystals. When they got there and showed Sadean's men that they possessed both the ring and the amulet, the men backed away and then fled. The three warriors were in awful shape from energy loss. The queen and Jared grabbed Ferulous first since he looked worst, dragging him into the color crystal tunnel. As soon as they did, Ferulous began to regain his life energy, and he was back to full energy in almost no time. The queen, Jared, and Ferulous then retrieved the other two warriors and dragged them to the color crystal tunnel as well. They all stayed there for several minutes, soaking in the life-giving energy of the crystals.

As the group was heading out of Dark Mountain, they noticed something on the ground. It was Olly. He had not survived the fight. He gave his life to save Jared. Jared picked Olly's lifeless body up to take with him so the little rock dragon could be buried at the palace. Jared was saddened by the loss of yet another friend.

The trip back to the palace was a long one. Sadean had stolen the queen's riding animal, so the queen and her companions all had to walk. It gave them a chance to talk about everything. Jared held out his hand to his mother. "What is it?" she asked. Jared dropped the ring into her hand. "You might have just saved the kingdom by getting this," the queen noted.

"Why is the ring so important?" Jared wanted to know.

"The ring or the amulet gives the wearer the power to help their people. When they are both worn by the same person, that power is nearly unlimited. Some day you will understand, my son."

"I think I already understand, Mom. Err . . . Your Majesty."

Queen Meriza, Jared, and the warriors talked the entire way back to the palace. When they got close, Jared got peculiarly quiet. "What is it now, Jared?"

"I'm just thinking about Princess Emera. I know it sounds stupid, but I think I'm in love with her."

"It doesn't sound stupid at all—not in Onteria. I know that you two were always meant to be together."

"But I'm still young."

"Age in Onteria means nothing. You've already grown up more in the past few days than you have over the entire last year."

Jared smiled and simply said, "Okay."

When the group arrived outside the palace, the twins came running out to greet the weary travelers. The girls were happier than ever to see their brother. Anna even said, "I'm glad you're alive!" to Jared. Then, they gave Jared and their mom big hugs.

"We need to be on our guard now that Sadean had his ring taken away," the queen warned everyone. "He will surely come back for it."

"Well then, Jared better have this," Ferulous said, holding out a sword to Jared with both hands. It was the sword that Sadean had been given by his father, Gregor, before Sadean used it to kill him. Ferulous had stolen it during the fight at Dark Mountain.

Jared looked at his mom with questioning eyes, and she gave him an approving look. "Thank you, Ferulous." Jared took the sword from him.

"Yes, thank you—all three of you," the queen added.

After everyone got settled back into the palace, Jared made plans to bury Olly out in the garden. He and Princess Emera dug Olly a resting spot and buried him that afternoon. They might not have gotten out of Dark Mountain if it wasn't for him. And he had definitely saved Jared's life.

That evening, at his mother's insistence, Jared met the queen in the palace library. The queen had the amulet around her neck and the ring in the palm of her hand. They were both glowing strongly. Then, she pulled them apart and handed the ring to Jared. "It's yours now," she said. "One day, I will teach you how to use it, and if you always keep it with you, it will protect you from harm. But for now, it's just a thing of beauty for you to wear." The queen knew it was risky to give the ring to her son since Sadean would surely come for it. But she thought it better to split the amulet and the ring up to lessen the chance of them both falling into Sadean's hands at once.

Chapter 11

Revenge

SADEAN WAS NOT ABOUT to let Jared go unpunished for taking his ring and getting his sword. He was back in Dark Mountain with some of his followers. Although some of Sadean's men had defected to Queen Meriza's side once they saw she was back in Onteria, and more had defected once they saw she possessed both the amulet and the ring, he still had a few loyal cohorts he could count on to help him capture and kill Jared. Some of those cohorts were, like the captain, palace spies. There were at least five of them Sadean knew he could count on.

This time, Sadean was angry enough that he intended to fulfill his original plan of attacking the palace directly. He was worried about getting past Hurstle and even more worried about the power of the amulet and the ring being together. But he figured his inside men could help on those fronts. He used the equivalent of a carrier pigeon to send one of his palace guard spies a message that simply read, *Prepare*. It was enough for the guard to know who it was from and what it meant.

Hurstle slept little, knowing that it was only a matter of time before Sadean or his followers would appear again. Hurstle roamed the palace at night, making sure the guards were in their positions and not sleeping. Most of the guards were intimidated by Hurstle. They could tell from his great size and his stern and confident attitude that he was not someone to mess around with. He was loyal to the queen and would give his life if it meant saving her or her family. The palace guards were glad to have Hurstle on their side—all except for the five Sadean had stationed there, that is.

As for Jonaria and Ferulous, the were getting attached to Jared and the twins. Jonaria reveled in her new duty of protecting the sisters. And Ferulous and Jared had a close connection with each other ever since Ferulous gifted Jared the tooth from the dead beast. Ferulous looked after Jared like he was the son he never had, and Jared looked to Ferulous as a kind of stand-in father since his real father had been killed. Though they had known each other only a short time, they had been through a lot together, and their bond was unbreakable. Ferulous slept in the room across from Jared's with a knife under his pillow and a sword propped up next to the bed so that he could protect Jared at a moment's notice.

That night, Queen Meriza, Jared, and the twins sat in the library, enjoying each other's company. They were glad to be together again as a family. But then, Hurstle walked in with a serious look on his face. "I'm sorry to interrupt you, but I have a bad feeling about tonight. I'm going to post more guards in the hallways and at the front gates." The queen nodded her agreement, and Hurstle left to do the deed.

The queen decided to use the brief moment of peace and calm to tell Jared more about the ring and what it could do. "One thing it can do is warn you of danger, like the Incognal did. Keep the ring on you at all times, and it will keep you safe."

Jared immediately slipped the ring onto his finger so that it sat on top of and snuggly against the ring that Princess Emera had gifted him during his first trips to Onteria. "It didn't keep Sadean safe, though," Jared pointed out.

"Sadean went looking for trouble and found it. Your job is to avoid trouble. And the ring will help you do that."

"Can Stephany and I sleep in your room tonight, Mom?" Anna asked. The twins were scared and did not want to be alone in their big rooms on such a dangerous evening.

"Yes, of course," the queen agreed.

After Jared went to his room and the queen and twins went to her room, Hurstle walked the palace's hallways with his two warrior companions. The inside guards that had helped Sadean set up his attack had no idea what to do. They had no way of informing Sadean that Hurstle had increased the number of guards and was standing guard himself. As the warriors roamed the halls, Hurstle spoke with the guards one by one and noticed that one guard seemed particularly nervous. "What's wrong? Why are you acting funny?" Hurstle asked the man.

When the guard began sweating, Hurstle knew for certain that something was not right. Hurstle leaned in toward the guard with a grimace on his face. He towered over the guard by at a least a head and a half. He pulled out a knife as he got closer and closer to the guard and asked him again, "Why are you so nervous?"

The guard finally cracked and revealed that Sadean was planning to attack the palace in the early morning hours. Hurstle was furious. He grabbed the guard and threw him to the floor, then put a knife to the guard's throat and asked, "Why are you supporting Sadean?"

"He has threatened to kill my parents if I don't assist him."

"How many other guards does he have here?"

The guard was hesitant to say. So, Hurstle pushed the knife against his throat with enough pressure to draw blood but not enough to cut it. "Five!" the guard finally blurted out.

"You are going to tell me exactly who they are," Hurstle demanded.

The guard agreed to help Hurstle identify the traitors. As Hurstle and the guard walked the halls, the guard would secretly signal to Hurstle if a guard they passed was a supporter of Sadean. When they were all done identifying Sadean's two other guards in the palace, they moved to the outside posts, where they identified Sadean's two remaining guards. After rounding up all five of the traitors, Hurstle positioned the original guard at an outside post where Sadean and his men would see him and not suspect anything. "If you alert anyone, I will personally rip your throat out," Hurstle warned the guard. The guard knew Hurstle was not joking, and he planned to do as he was told.

Hurstle alerted Jonaria and Ferulous to the situation. But they decided not to alert the royal family for fear of unnecessarily scaring them. It was almost midnight. The warriors were sure that Sadean would be attacking soon.

The guard that informed Hurstle about the other guards who were supporters of Sadean missed two more that even he didn't know about. There was another turncoat guard stationed outside the palace, and Sadean had a steward inside who could move about the palace freely without causing suspicion. The steward was Sadean's most trusted man inside the palace, and he had not even revealed himself to Sadean's other supporters there.

Jared could not get to sleep, so he got up to get a drink of water. He ran into the steward in the kitchen. "What are you doing up at this late hour with so much danger afoot?" the steward asked.

"Just getting a drink of water is all. And then, I'll go straight back to my room."

"Let me prepare something for you that will help you sleep," the steward insisted. He prepared a drink and a lite snack for Jared. But he added a dash of wildflower seeds that dissolved in the liquid. "Go ahead and try it," he urged.

Jared, having no reason to suspect anything from a trustworthy steward within the palace walls, took a big gulp of the drink. He then ate the snack and took another big gulp of the drink. That was the last thing Jared remembered. He didn't make it out of the kitchen on his own. The wildflower seeds were a quick-acting poison that would render a person unconscious in small doses but kill them in larger doses. The steward knew that Sadean wanted to kill Jared himself, so he used a smaller dose of the poison. As Jared began to pass out, the steward caught his goblet before it could clang to the floor.

The steward laid Jared on a serving cart, covered him with

a cloth, and then wheeled him to a back door of the palace. There, Sadean's one remaining outside guard who had not been found out yet took the cart and began wheeling it toward the palace gates. When he got to the gates, a guard asked him, "What do you have there?"

"Just some refreshments for the men standing guard outside."

"Very well. Proceed. But make it quick!" the queen's guard insisted. He opened the gate for Sadean's guard, and then he quickly shut it.

Sadean's men arrived outside the palace gate, disguised as local merchants. They took Jared, now wrapped in the sheet, and loaded him onto the back of their pack animal that resembled a horse but was much bigger.

Hurstle, Ferulous, and Jonaria stayed ready for battle throughout the night, but nothing ever happened. The next morning, when the royal family got up, they headed to the dining room to eat. When they noticed that everyone in the family but Jared had shown up, Stephany said she would go wake him. But Ferulous told her no and insisted that he would go do it. Stephany agreed.

Hurstle entered the dining room. "Did anything happen last night, Hurstle?" the queen asked him.

"No, Your Majesty. Everything was peaceful. I'm surprised."

"I'm surprised, too." The queen looked concerned.

Ferulous reentered the dining room and announced, "Jared is not in his room. Do you think he went for a walk with Princess Emera?"

Almost on cue, the princess entered the dining room next. Now, the queen was *extremely* concerned. When the steward brought in everyone's food, she asked him, "Have you seen my son, Jared, this morning?"

"Yes, My Queen. I saw him taking a walk this morning," the steward lied. "He was outside the palace but within the palace walls."

Despite the steward's assertion that Jared was on the palace grounds, Hurstle had a bad feeling. He called Jonaria to the dining room and told everyone there that he, Ferulous, and Jonaria would walk the palace inside and out looking for Jared. As they searched the palace and grounds, they stopped every guard and asked them if they had seen Jared. Hurstle then approached the Sadean-loyal guard he had interrogated the night before and began questioning him again. "I thought you told me there would be an attack last night. What happened?"

"I don't know. The message I received from Sadean said there would be an attack. So, there should have been one."

Hurstle grunted in disapproval and then walked off. He and the other two warriors continued to search the palace and surrounding grounds for Jared. Then, they returned to the dining room and announced that Jared was gone without a trace.

Chapter 12

Master Plan

SADEAN NOW HAD JARED, but Jared had not yet woken up from being drugged. Sadean was getting impatient while waiting for him to wake up. Back at the palace, the queen was impatient, too. She anxiously awaited any news of her son's whereabouts. "He could not have vanished without a trace. Someone must know what happened to him," she implored.

Hurstle, Ferulous, and Jonaria were investigating Jared's disappearance by questioning all the guards and staff. Hurstle returned to the Sadean-loyal guard once more. "You know more than you're telling me. Tell me everything," Hurstle demanded. "Where is the queen's son?"

The guard was extremely nervous and intimidated. "I told you everything I know!" he blurted out.

"I don't believe you. Maybe some time in the dungeon will help you think of something helpful to tell me." The palace guards helped round up all of the Sadean-loyal guards and locked them in a room with the three warriors. There was a feeling of tension in the room that gave the guards anxiety. "Where . . . is . . . *Jared*?!" Hurstle yelled at the guards.

The guards jumped in fear. One of the guards looked even more nervous and fearful than the rest. Hurstle approached him and looked him directly in the eyes. Hurstle then nodded to Jonaria, who grabbed the guard by both arms and dragged him to another room so he could be interrogated in private.

Hurstle continued to spin around the room, glaring at the guards and causing them to feel uncomfortable. When one of the guards cleared his throat, the warriors dragged that guard to another room for interrogation as well. Hurstle left the rest of the guards in the first room, locked it, and put extra palace guards in place outside the door. "No one leaves, and no one talks," Hurstle instructed. The palace guards nodded in understanding.

When Hurstle exited the room, he noticed the palace steward scurrying away down the hall. He found it odd that the steward was in that wing of the palace at that time of day. Hurstle made a mental note of it and then entered the room where Jonaria was holding one of the Sadean-loyal guards. Hurstle approached the guard, looked him directly in the eyes, and asked, "Where is Jared?" This time, Hurstle's voice was calm but demanding.

The guard stuttered out, "I-I-I had nothing to do with Jared's disappearance! All I know is that there w-w-was supposed to be an attack on the p-p-palace last night."

"Are there any conspirators in the palace other than the guards we've already rounded up?" Hurstle demanded to know. Hurstle noticed the guard had wet himself and knew he was talking to the right person. "Well? Out with it!" he demanded.

"One . . . of the . . . head stewards . . . is Sadean's m-m-man," the guard struggled to get out.

"Which one?"

"The . . . headmaster."

Hurstle immediately knew which steward it was as he had just seen the man attempting to eavesdrop moments earlier. He gathered the warriors, and they went to the headmaster's quarters and searched his room. There, they found the container of wildflower seeds used to make the drug Jared had ingested. "Let's split up and search the palace for him," Hurstle suggested.

The palace was enormous, with many places to hide, especially for someone like the headmaster steward who was so familiar with it. So, the warriors enlisted their loyal palace guards to help look for him. While the guards searched the palace, Hurstle and Jonaria informed the queen of the unfolding events. "We know who was involved in Jared's disappearance," Jonaria told her. "It was the headmaster steward."

The queen gasped. "He was just here to bring us a fresh pot of tea!"

Seeing Anna about to take a sip of the tea, Hurstle swatted it away from her. Jonaria lifted the teapot lid and took in a big whiff. "It's laced with wildflower seed and a generous amount of it!" Jonaria announced. "There's not enough to kill you, but you all would have been out cold until tomorrow."

Hurstle and Jonaria looked at each other with sternness. "Let's find him!" Hurstle said. "Lock the door behind us, Your Majesty. Do not let anyone in until we get back." After walking out of the room, Hurstle and Jonaria heard a lock on the door engage. "Follow me!" Hurstle insisted. They were off to visit the original guard they had interrogated, who had, by now, been moved to the dungeon.

When Hurstle and Jonaria reached the dungeon, they were dismayed to discover that the cell the guard had been held in was empty and its door was open. It was another inside job. "He's probably fled the palace grounds by now and is on his way to Sadean," Jonaria pointed out. Hurstle nodded his head in agreement.

Hurstle, Ferulous, and Jonaria returned to the library. They were immediately alarmed when they discovered that the guards they had stationed outside the door were no longer there. Ferulous knocked on the door, and he heard a meek and shaky voice answer with, "Who is it?" It was Anna, but she sounded worried.

"It's us, Hurstle and Jonaria," Hurstle answered. "Unlock the door and let us in."

"I can't. The lock is . . . stuck," Anna replied.

Hurstle and Jonaria had not heard Anna even try to disengage the lock. They now knew for sure that something was not right. "Okay, we'll just come back," Hurstle lied. He waited a few moments until he was sure that Anna was free of the door on the other side. Then, he backed up to the other side of the hallway, opposite the door, as far as he could. He charged the door, and with one hit from the enormous Hurstle, the door buckled and caved in. When the three warriors rushed into the library, there stood the headmaster steward and the first Sadean-loyal guard they had discovered. The headmaster had a knife to the queen's throat, and the guard had the twins by their arms.

"Let them go!" Hurstle demanded.

"Come any closer, and the queen will die," the steward warned Hurstle.

As Ferulous stood behind Hurstle, partially shielded from view, he slowly withdrew a knife from his back sheath. Hurstle heard the distinctive sound of the knife coming out of the sheath and leaned to his left. As he did so, a knife went whirring past his head and embedded directly into the headmaster's throat, causing him to drop to the ground. Jonaria ran to the queen and pulled her to safety.

Ferulous withdrew another knife and turned in the guard's direction. The guard, stunned by Ferulous's skills with the knife and afraid for his life, put his hands up and pleaded, "Don't kill me!"

"Tell us where they took Jared, and we will let you live," Ferulous said.

"Sadean has an outpost on the outskirts of the desert," the guard informed the warriors. "Since you already discovered his lair in Dark Mountain, I'm guessing they took Jared to that outpost instead."

Hurstle instructed Ferulous to get a map from the library. Ferulous returned within a few minutes. "Show me on the map where Sadean is hiding out," Hurstle demanded. In response, the guard pointed to a location on the map that was beyond Dark Mountain, just past the desert springs. It was at least an entire day trip to get there with the use of pack animals.

The warriors called the palace guards they knew they could trust and handed their prisoner over to them. The guards returned him to the dungeon. He was placed in his own cell with four palace guards standing watch this time. There was little chance of another escape.

The queen was informed of Jared's likely whereabouts. Hurstle said, "My team and I can prepare for the trip and be off within an hour. You need to stay here with the amulet. Now that Sadean has his ring again, we cannot risk your life or the amulet falling to him."

Queen Meriza nodded her agreement. "Bring my son back to me, Hurstle."

"We will not fail you, Your Majesty," Hurstle confirmed.

The three warriors gathered their gear and headed to the stable to prepare their pack animals. Once the animals were loaded up, the warriors climbed onto them, and they were off. Ferulous carried the map and led the way to the desert. It would be a rough trip through steep terrain for the animals and would push them to their limits.

Once the warriors reached the highest elevation of their trip, they made camp for the night and let the animals rest. They unloaded their gear and laid out their bedding to sleep on. After a quick meal, they fell fast asleep. As warriors, they were purposefully light sleepers and were not worried about anyone sneaking up on them in the middle of the night.

The warriors were up and repacked by first light. Hurstle estimated they would make it past the desert springs by mid-day. Even though they had a ways to go before they reached Sadean's outpost, they knew they had to be stealthy in case Sadean had lookouts posted along the way. The terrain on the rest of the journey would not be as bad as before, so the pack animals would be able to travel further in less time.

When the warriors made it to the springs, they filled up their water jugs and let the animals drink. From that point on, the warriors would be on foot, and the animals would be left at the springs, waiting for them. Everyone was eager to see Jared's condition and confirm whether he was even still alive.

After another hour of walking while keeping a low profile, it was late afternoon. The warriors came upon a rocky location where the rocks had clearly been modified. There were no guards out front, but the warriors could hear voices echoing from within a cavern. They also heard Jared screaming for help and Sadean telling him to remain quiet. The warriors knew they were in the right place and were happy to know that Jared was still alive. But they could tell from his screams that they needed to rescue him as soon as possible.

"Why are they keeping him alive?" Hurstle wondered aloud.

"Because they don't have *this* yet," Ferulous responded. He held out his arm so the others could see the ring that was sitting in the palm of his hand. "Jared feared that he would be recaptured by Sadean, so he gave the ring to me for safekeeping, knowing that nobody would suspect I have it."

"Why did you bring it with you?" Jonaria asked. "Now, Sadean is closer to getting it than he was before."

"I figured it would help guide us to Sadean's new lair if we couldn't find it on our own and that it would protect us once we got there," Ferulous explained.

"Well, it's certainly a risky move," Hurstle noted. "I guess we'll find out how risky soon enough. I'm just thankful that Jared had the good sense to give the ring up when he did. It's the only reason he's alive right now."

Hurstle led the way into the caverns that served as Sadean's new lair. Despite their enormous sizes, the warriors were able to tread lightly enough that their footsteps did not echo and give their presence away. After a series of twists and turns through a long corridor, the warriors eventually made it to an opening at the center of the outpost. They could tell that they were now deep underground as there had been a tremendous drop in temperature. And they knew they were getting closer to Jared because his screams were getting louder.

Suddenly, the warriors heard men yelling and an army of footsteps. "They're coming this way!" Jonaria whisper-shouted in alarm. "There's no place for us to hide. We'll need to stand our ground." The warriors could now see the shadows of Sadean's men on the wall and knew they were moments away from a battle.

As Sadean's men came running around a corner, the first few men ran directly into Hurstle, who found himself facing the tip of a spear. The men would have to get through Hurstle first, which they knew would not be easy. Hurstle was a mean fighter, and he took up most of the space in the corridor. He raised his sword and swung it, stopping Sadean's men in their path and causing them to back up a few feet. Ferulous with his knives and Jonaria with her arrows stood at the ready behind Hurstle.

The man with the spear thrust it at Hurstle, and the fight was on. Knives were furiously flying from behind Hurstle and embedding in Sadean's men. Then, the arrows started and took down several more men. Blood was pouring throughout the corridor, but it was all from the opposing side. Sadean's men were no match for Hurstle and his team of warriors. The men knew it, and Sadean knew it, which is why Sadean's voice suddenly called out, "Stop fighting! Everyone!"

Ferulous yelled to the other warriors, "We mustn't stop now! Kill as many men as you can while we have the upper hand!" He threw another knife, which struck a man standing right next to Sadean himself.

"This bloodshed is unnecessary," Sadean insisted. "All I want is my ring back. I'm the rightful owner of it. Nobody else. If you give me the ring, I'll give you Jared."

Hurstle pulled back his sword, ready to strike down Sadean. But as Sadean stepped out of the shadows, Hurstle could see that Sadean was with Jared and had a knife to Jared's throat. "Stop fighting, or I will kill Jared now," Sadean warned. With Jared being one of the few pure bloods left in line for the throne, the warriors knew they couldn't take the chance, and so they yielded . . . for the moment.

"We yield for now," Hurstle announced. "But only for so long as you don't harm Jared. One drop of blood from him, and we will wipe out your entire army, and you will never see the ring again."

Sadean repeated his demands. "Give me the ring, and I will put my blade down." He knew that Jared didn't have the ring on him but didn't know that Ferulous had it. Instead, he figured it had been hidden somewhere within the palace. "Go get me the ring and be back by the day after tomorrow," Sadean told the warriors. "Only then will I release Jared to you."

As the conversation was taking place, Sadean's men had

somewhat regrouped, and they now stood shoulder to shoulder, creating a barricade around Sadean. Although the warriors were certain they could cut Sadean's men down completely, they worried about what that might mean for Jared's life. Hurstle looked at his companions and said, "Let's back out. But watch for a trap."

The warriors knew they didn't need to return to the palace for the ring. So, once they had exited the cavern outpost, they made a new plan. To make Sadean's men think they were returning to the palace, the warriors backtracked all the way to the pack animals they had left at the desert springs. They would camp there for the night and resume their quest in the morning.

Sadean, knowing the warriors likely had no intention of retrieving the ring and that they would need to bed down somewhere for the night, decided that this was his best chance to remove them from the picture once and for all. He had hired the best mercenaries in the region and told them to attack and overwhelm the warriors as they slept, as it would be the only time Sadean's men would stand a chance against them. The warriors were the main thing standing between Sadean and the throne.

Chapter 13

Double-Cross

SADEAN WAS NOT CONFIDENT in his decision to attack the warriors as they slept, but he knew he had to take the chance. He positioned his mercenaries outside the warriors' camp, ready to attack from all directions. The killers had knives, swords, arrows, and various hand-to-hand weapons in case the fighting moved to close combat. But before they were ready to attack, there was suddenly a loud squawking sound that woke the warriors. It was a rock dragon that had been startled by the men creeping around.

The mercenaries began their attack prematurely, sending arrows flying past Jonaria. Within milliseconds, the warriors sprung to their feet with weapons in hand, ready for a fight. A dozen mercenary fighters came out of the darkness and were lit up by the glow from the camp's fire. The men were dressed in all black, with their faces covered with scarves. It was four of them to every one warrior. But Hurstle loved a good fight!

Arrows and knives were flying through the air in all directions while swords clanked together. Jonaria yelled as she was pinned down by six men at once. With her being the smallest warrior, though not small and not weak, the men hoped to take her out first. With Hurstle and Ferulous preoccupied with the remaining men, they could not help Jonaria out. Jonaria was dragged off until the remaining two warriors could no longer hear her screams.

The remaining mercenaries were no match for the hulking warriors, especially Hurstle, who made even Ferulous look small. One by one, the men in black were falling, and as fast as the fight began, it was over. The two victors stood in the middle of all the men lying on the ground as the rock dragon continued to squawk in the background. Then, the dragon stopped squawking, attached itself to Ferulous's leg, and began purring. "Looks like you have a new friend," Hurstle noted.

"If he chose me, I guess I have to keep him," Ferulous agreed. "I'll call him Slag."

"Which way did they take Jonaria? Did you see?"

"No!"

The two warriors headed back to Sadean's rocky outpost. Given the sparse desert terrain around them, they figured there was nowhere else Sadean's mercenaries could have taken Jonaria. It was still dark out, so it made the conditions perfect for Hurstle and Ferulous to sneak back into the cavern undetected. But it was so dark that they had difficulty seeing while within the cavern, too. Slag was right at home. But the warriors had to use light crystals they had brought to see the way.

There was an eerie quiet within the corridors of the outpost. Hurstle and Ferulous wondered why nobody had confronted them yet. They also wondered why they couldn't hear

Jonaria as they assumed she would put up a relentless fight. But there was nothing—almost no sound at all.

Eventually, Hurstle and Ferulous made it to the opening where they had earlier fought Sadean's men. Other than the blood-spattered ground, walls, and even ceiling of the opening, there was no sign of Sadean's men there. The warriors continued through the corridors until they began to see light. They had reached the other side of the outpost without finding a single soul. When they exited out into the desert, they realized that they had been in the outpost for hours and that it was now midmorning. Sadean and his horde of men, along with Jared and Jonaria, had vanished. The warriors were concerned and furious.

Chapter 14

The Search

WITH SO MANY of Sadean's men having fled in such a short time, there was no way for them to cover their tracks in the sand. Following the footprints was a natural starting point for Hurstle and Ferulous as they tried to track down their missing companions. The tracks went in several different directions, which was clearly a deliberate attempt by Sadean to throw the warriors off. But Hurstle recognized Jonaria's footprints, which were much larger than the rest. "Looks like she made it this far!" Hurstle pointed out with hope in his voice. "She's a fighter."

Slag had flown a few feet ahead of the warriors and was squawking, indicating that he wanted them to follow him. In addition to their other admirable qualities, rock dragons had keen senses for tracking people. Slag was naturally following the footprints as well, and it seemed that he might know which set of prints would lead the warriors to Sadean's men.

After the warriors and slag followed the footprints for around two hours, the prints suddenly disappeared. There were no tracks leading in any direction. Slag veered off to the right and began squawking for the warriors to follow him. "It looks like Slag knows the way they went," Ferulous suggested. So, the warriors continued to follow him.

Sadean was in his preferred location: another underground tunnel system. He had planned all along for the warriors to follow the footprints so that he could then erase them and leave the warriors stranded in the middle of the desert. He had not anticipated a rock dragon attaching itself to one of the warriors. But with Jared and Jonaria both tied up in his new location as bargaining chips, Sadean figured he still had the upper hand in the situation.

Every time Jared or Jonaria tried to talk, Sadean's men threw rocks at them to keep them quiet. The men did not want Hurstle and Ferulous hearing them. Jonaria lowered her voice and whispered to Jared, "Can you reach my boot? I'm too tied up."

"Yes," Jared confirmed.

"Wait until the guards are not looking. Then, I'll remove my boot. There's a knife at the bottom. I need you to grab it."

At an opportune time, Jared did just that. And he knew what to do with the knife without being told. He cut Jonaria's ties. Then, Jonaria took the knife and cut Jared free. Now freed, they held their same positions so that the guards wouldn't notice. "Ask one of them to come give you a drink of water," Jonaria instructed Jared. She knew that until Sadean had the ring, they wanted to keep Jared alive and well. Jonaria and Jared were, in fact, so parched that their mouths were dry, and their lips were white and cracking, which helped sell the ruse.

"Some water please?" Jared called out to one of Sadean's men. Without questioning Jared's intentions, the man brought water to him.

"Don't give any to the woman," one of Sadean's other guards called out. Jonaria was not as important to them, so they didn't care as much about her wellbeing. They planned to kill her as soon as they had word from Sadean. Although Sadean wanted her dead, he was still considering whether she could be used to lure the other warriors to their deaths as well.

Sadean was also cooking up other plans. He was grasping at straws for any way he could take the throne and wondered whether he could entice Jared to take a place by his side in exchange for him convincing his mother to retire the crown. He knew the queen would never agree to it if Sadean made the offer himself, but he wondered whether Jared could convince her. With Queen Meriza on her throne and with two warriors in pursuit of his head, Sadean was getting desperate. He was beginning to feel that he couldn't even fully trust his own followers. They were mostly comprised of killers, thieves, and mercenaries. There were only a few loyal followers, and they were only followers of Sadean because they were attracted to power like he was and would do anything to get more of it.

Sadean ordered one of his henchmen to bring Jared to him. Two guards went to retrieve Jared, but when they entered the area where Jared and Jonaria should have been, the captives were gone. There was just one guard there, and he was tied up on the ground. The captives had vanished, but Sadean knew they could not have gone far in the desert. Their best bet would have been to stay within the cool temperatures of the tunnel system, which was so vast that if someone didn't know where they were going, they could roam around for days without finding an exit. Sadean didn't care about Jonaria, but he could not afford to have Jared perish.

Chapter 15

The Maze

THE ROCK DRAGON GUIDED Hurstle and Ferulous to Sadean's new location. They would never have found it if it were not for Slag. As they entered the rock formations in the sand, they did so with caution. They were aware that if Jonaria had been taken prisoner instead of killed that it could be a trap to lure them in.

The corridors that the warriors now found themselves in seemed devoid of men. But there were wild beasts down there that hunted the desert for food at night. Hurstle and Ferulous had heard legends about the desert beasts, and they came prepared, bringing certain wildflowers with them on their journey to stave the beasts off. If someone carried this type of flower with them, then a beast could be standing right next to them, and all it would smell is the flower.

Jonaria had also heard about the desert beasts. She knew that she and Jared could not safely find an exit from the under-ground tunnels without the help of someone who knew where one was and how to avoid the beasts. So, Jonaria and Jared crouched behind some rocks, ready to capture and interrogate one of the guards that were now coming after them.

Sadean was growing impatient that it was taking the guards so long to bring Jared to him. So, he went to check on his prisoners himself. When he discovered that they had escaped, he was furious. The guard that Jared and Jonaria had tied up asked Sadean to untie him. In response, Sadean drove a sword through the man's chest and held it there long enough to kill him. Then, Sadean cursed himself for not killing Jonaria himself when he had the chance. He was right back to having three warriors on the loose and no ring.

It was not long before a guard came wandering by Jared and Jonaria. He was easily subdued by Jonaria. He was frightened by the great warrior and agreed without hesitation to guide her and Jared to an exit. But they would have to walk a long way to get there.

As for Hurstle, Ferulous, and Slag, they made it through the first couple of tunnels safely. They were now in what appeared to be a main tunnel, which had several turnoffs they could choose from. Slag could smell people. He turned to the left, and he and the warriors went down a corridor that seemed to get narrower the further they went down it. "Are you sure you know where you're going, Slag?" Ferulous asked. Slag just squawked and kept going down the tunnel. Ferulous shrugged and followed behind.

The warriors were thankful they still had their crystal lights with them because they certainly could not see as well as a rock dragon could. As the tunnel they were in got smaller, especially for Hurstle, Ferulous called out to Slag again, "Do you know where you're going?" Slag stopped and squeaked lightly. The two warriors stopped behind him. They froze and listened intently. They heard heavy guttural breathing coming from behind them. It was a beast that had been tracking them.

The warriors pulled out their weapons and prepared for a fight. "Is there a different way we can go, Slag?" Ferulous asked. But there was no sound from the rock dragon. The dragon was intently focused on trying to track the beast's location to see how close it was to them.

The beast's breathing got louder, but it echoed in all directions down in the tunnel, so no one was sure which direction the beast might be coming from. Suddenly, there was a growl. "It's right behind us!" Hurstle yelled out. Both warriors turned around in the small corridor they were in, hoping that they had enough room to fight the beast. But before they could react, Slag pushed his way between them and let out a high-pitched scream. The warriors' ears were ringing, and they felt dizzy. The scream was used by some rock dragons to disorient an opponent so the dragon could get the upper hand.

There was another growl from the beast, but this time it was the pained growl of an injured animal. The warriors tried to use their light crystals to see what was happening but were unable to make anything out. Then, they heard heavy, stomping feet in the tunnel as the beast ran off. Slag had saved their lives.

Hurstle looked at Ferulous, and they both let out a sigh of relief as they put away their weapons. Fighting a beast and fighting a person were two very different things. Though they were confident they could always defeat a person, they were never so sure when it came to beasts. They considered themselves lucky to be alive. Slag pushed his way through the two of them, making his way to the front again, ready to lead. "Lead the way, Slag!" Ferulous called out with a chuckle. A squawk is all he heard in response.

The guard that Jared and Jonaria had captured knew that if he made it back to Sadean empty-handed, Sadean would kill him. So, he figured his best bet for staying alive would be to help them find an exit to flee through and then flee himself—if, that is, he was lucky enough to have Jonaria let him live. While Hurstle and Ferulous were trying to head deeper into the tunnels, Jared and Jonaria were trying to head out.

Chapter 16

The Queen

Q UEEN MERIZA, her daughters, and Princess Emera were
still at the palace. They had loyal palace guards all around
them in case any of Sadean's men came back to grab one of
them. Though the queen was distraught, she stayed calm on the
surface, mostly as a beacon of confidence for her twins and
Emera. "As long as we stay here at the palace, everything will
be fine," the queen assured everyone. She truly was a great
leader. To further keep the twins calm, the queen even had the
palace cook prepare their favorite: strawberry shortcake—or at
least, the Onterian version of it.

The queen desired to confront the guards that had betrayed
her. Since they were locked in the dungeon and she was stuck
at the palace, she figured it was the only thing she could do to
help combat Sadean for the time being. As she made her way
to the dungeon, she became more agitated and angry.

When the queen entered the cell block, she stood quietly
for several moments, trying to collect herself before saying
anything. The originally-discovered Sadean-loyal guard, who

she had known since she was a teenager, stood there in front of her, behind a wall of bars. "Why did you betray me?" Meriza asked. "I've known you all my life. And you've known my family all yours." The guard stood there without a word. "Answer me!" the queen demanded.

"I'm sorry, My Queen. Sadean threatened to kill my parents if I did not help him. With you having left the kingdom, I had nobody here to protect me. Princess Emera is not as strong as you are and could not possibly be up to the task. I felt threatened by Sadean and abandoned by you. I can still be loyal to you, but I'm afraid you'll just abandon us again."

"All you had to do was follow Princess Emera in my stead. Now, thanks to you, my son is missing and in Sadean's grasp—possibly even dead. Sadean wants to rule this kingdom and all known worlds with an iron fist, and you've helped him get closer to doing that."

"I can give you information in exchange for my freedom," the guard offered. "It will allow you to trust me again."

"What could you possibly offer me that Hurstle was not able to get out of you?"

"I can tell you something about Sadean that you don't know because you were gone for so many years."

"What information do you have about Sadean that would be worth your freedom?"

"Agree to set me free first, and I will tell you. The information I have is well worth it. If your son is still alive, it could help save his life." The guard hoped that appealing to the queen's love for her son would aid him in getting what he wanted.

The queen told the guard she would think about it and let him know within the hour. Throughout the rest of that hour, she pondered what kind of information the guard could possibly have on Sadean. And if Hurstle, the most intimidating warrior in Onteria, could not get that information out of the guard, why would he so freely offer it up to her? After thinking it over, she finally made a decision and returned to the guard's cell. "Because we're talking about my son's life, I will take the gamble and set you free in exchange for the information you can offer about Sadean," the queen said. "So, start talking."

"Sadean does not want the power of the ring and the amulet just to allow him to be an all-powerful ruler. He is also gravely ill and has discovered a way to infuse the power of the stones into his body to help him heal."

"What kind of sickness are we talking about?" the queen prodded.

"For the rest of the information, you'll need to set me free first," the guard countered.

The queen looked toward the dungeon guards and told them to set the Sadean-loyal guard free. They did as they were told, and the guard walked out. The queen and the palace guards escorted the man to the palace gates. There, he finished providing the queen with the information she needed.

"Sadean has a *mental* sickness," the guard explained. "He is going mad and seeing things that are not really there. He believes he still sees your father, Gregor, even though Gregor died over one hundred years ago. And he believes Gregor is the one instructing him to take over the kingdom. The sickness is the only reason he turned evil and is doing what he's doing."

153

The queen was at a loss for words. "Does he really believe what he is seeing?"

"Yes," the guard confirmed.

"Is there anything else you can tell me?"

"No."

"Then, you are free to leave the palace grounds. But you will never work in the palace or even in this city again."

The palace gates opened, and the Sadean-loyal guard scurried through them and quickly walked away, out of view. As he left, he shed a tear of shame. He would never be seen within the city of Onteria again.

Queen Meriza returned to the library, where her daughters and the princess had remained. She had been gone for so long that they were worried something bad had happened to her. She assured everyone that everything was fine and that they would get Jared back. She knew Sadean would need Jared as a bargaining chip and wouldn't kill him unless Sadean had at least the ring.

At that same moment, one of Sadean's men was escorting Jared and Jonaria toward an exit from Sadean's latest hideout while Jonaria held a knife to his back. By now, the other guards had informed Sadean that their partner was missing. Sadean became enraged and yelled out, "Find him! And when you do, kill him! Bring the other two to me."

Chapter 17

Madness

S ADEAN'S MENTAL HEALTH was getting worse by the
day. If he did not infuse himself with the power of the
stones soon, he would go completely mad, and nobody would
follow him anymore. He desperately needed the stones back.
He still couldn't believe that he went from having one of the
stones to having none. As the queen had predicted, Jared was
going to be Sadean's leverage to get the amulet from the queen.
But now, Jared was gone as well.

For fifteen years, Sadean had been looking for a place
known as the heart of the Caverns of Olna. The heart was
where the jewels from which the amulet and ring were made
came from. It was said that the heart is where the true power of
Onteria lies. But Olna Mountain keeps it hidden and protected.
Sadean had hoped his ring would be enough to guide him to the
heart, but it was not strong enough on its own. Sadean needed
the amulet as well. Only then would he have enough power to
locate the heart, where he hoped to locate more healing stones.

Sadean's visions had started decades earlier, and they were

always the same. His father, Gregor, was the main focus of the living dreams. Sometimes, Sadean's visions were so vivid that he couldn't tell what was real and what was imagined. It was part of what fueled the intense anger within him.

As Sadean was waiting for the guards to deliver Jared to him, he was in the middle of another vision. In this one, Sadean's father was telling him that he was not as strong as his sister. Sadean grew enraged with jealousy and killed his father all over again by plunging an imaginary sword into the imaginary Gregor. Sadean's mind was almost completely gone.

Chapter 18

The Ring

FERULOUS STILL HAD the ring with him. He planned to give it to Jared as soon as he found him. Sadean and his men were looking for Jared, as were Hurstle and Ferulous, and yet, no one could find him. The tunnels they were in were so vast that there seemed to be an almost endless combination of choices one could make on where to go. As for Sadean, he still had a strong bond with the ring, and he could sense it was close. He headed into the tunnels to follow his senses and find it.

Jonaria pleaded with Jared to keep up with her and their captive guard. Jared was getting tired and lagging. He asked if they could take a break, but Jonaria insisted that they could not stop. She knew that by now, Sadean's men were likely searching the tunnels for them. They had to keep moving. Their lives depended on it—at least, Jonaria's did.

"Are we getting close to the exit?" Jonaria asked the guard.

"No. Not yet," the man replied.

"You better be taking us there and not in circles until the

others catch up with us." Jonaria gritted her teeth at the thought.

The guard smiled and said, "I guess you'll just need to trust me. My life is now at stake as much as yours is."

"Let's keep moving then," Jonaria insisted.

In another part of the tunnels, Slag had made about a dozen turns. Hurstle and Ferulous were completely lost, so they stuck close to the rock dragon. Eventually, they entered a cavern that was full of light crystals. Hurstle broke a few of them off a wall to give him and Ferulous some extra light in the tunnels. These were the brightest light crystals they had ever encountered, and they could see that the room they were in seemed to go on forever. It took them fifteen minutes to traverse the light crystal room.

Once Hurstle, Ferulous, and Slag exited the light crystal room, the walls around them changed to a glowing green and black crystal. The walls looked emerald, but with black mixed into the green. "I've heard legends about this tunnel," Ferulous said. "The legend says that the green and black walls can let you peer into your soul and show you your future. You have to stare directly into the walls with your hands resting on them."

"I've heard the stories as well," Hurstle confirmed. "I never thought they were real. But now, I'm starting to wonder."

"Stop for a moment, Slag," Ferulous called out. "Return to me." The rock dragon looked disappointed but returned to Ferulous's leg and began purring.

"What are you doing?" Hurstle asked.

"I want to try out the wall." Ferulous moved closer to the green and black wall and rested his hands against it. Then, he gazed deep into it. He became mesmerized by the smoky pattern in the green. He felt he was becoming hypnotized by it.

After a couple of minutes of watching Ferulous look into the wall, Hurstle called out, "Are you alright?" But there was no answer from Ferulous. Hurstle walked directly up to Ferulous so that the two men were just inches apart and asked again, "Are you alright?" Again, there was no answer. Hurstle rested his hand on Ferulous's shoulder, and Ferulous startled and jumped as if he were coming out of a nightmare. Hurstle looked straight into Ferulous's eyes. Ferulous's eyes were so big that there was only black in them. "What did you see?"

There was a long silence before Ferulous finally whispered, "I saw our future."

"And?" Hurstle prodded.

"And . . . we *fail*. Jared is killed. And Queen Meriza goes back into hiding with her daughters."

"Well, I'm sure we can just change that future," Hurstle suggested. "Whatever path you saw us taking in the wall, we'll just take a different one. It will have a different outcome. What path did the wall show us taking?"

Ferulous did not answer the question. Instead, he took a deep breath and said, "Slag, let's keep moving." Slag detached himself from Ferulous's leg and bounded out of the cavern of green jeweled walls. Ferulous and, more reluctantly, Hurstle followed behind. As they came to their first option to turn, Slag went right. "Stop!" Ferulous called out. "We need to go down this passageway instead," he said, motioning in a different direction. Slag did not seem happy about the course change. But as his two warrior companions moved toward the new walkway, he rushed past them to take the lead again.

Jonaria was suspicious of the route she was on as well. She was beginning to trust the guard guiding them less and less. Suddenly, they heard voices nearby. "Stop!" Jonaria called out to Jared and the guard in a whisper. "Someone's coming."

Jared's heart started pounding. He could hear it in his ears. "Can we go back the other way?" he asked, motioning to where they had just come from. But then, they heard voices coming from that direction as well.

"We're over here!" the guard suddenly blurted out.

Jonaria was furious. She punched the guard, knocking him out—more to keep him quiet than because of her anger. But it was too late. Jonaria and Jared now heard the sounds of footsteps running toward them. Within a few moments, Sadean's men surrounded and detained them. Sadean's men dragged Jared away, and Jonaria could hear him yelling, "Let me go!" with his voice getting dimmer and dimmer.

One of Sadean's men bent down and cut the throat of the guard who was helping Jared and Jonaria find an exit. "How could you do that to one of your own?" Jonaria asked.

"He was weak," the killer responded. "Sadean does not tolerate weakness. And now, it's *your* turn to die!"

Jonaria was surrounded by five men of fairly large stature. They all had knives and swords on them, and all she had in her hand was the small knife that she and Jared had used to cut themselves free. She knew she would be no match for them. But she was determined that if she was going to go down, she was going to take one or two of Sadean's men with her.

One of Sadean's men immediately grabbed Jonaria's throat

and began choking her. He was so big that she was lifted into the air by his powerful arms. Then, two men tried to grab her arms. But before they could do so, Jonaria thrust her knife deep into the inner thigh of the man holding her. It was a precision jab that cut the man's artery. He dropped Jonaria and quickly bled to death. At almost the same time, a fourth man thrust a large knife toward Jonaria's throat. It cut her fairly deep but not deep enough to kill her.

Suddenly, Hurstle appeared and attacked. Within no time, he had taken out four of the five men attacking Jonaria. But the fifth man held a knife against Jonaria and moved behind her to use her as a shield. Ferulous, who had taken a different tunnel than Hurstle, emerged behind the man and crept up to him. He expertly thrust his knife into the side of the man holding Jonaria and twisted the knife around to keep the wound from closing up. Jonaria was free.

Hurstle, Ferulous, and Jonaria stood around for a moment surveying the carnage around them. The bodies of Sadean's men would eventually be devoured by the beasts that roamed the tunnels. "It's good to see you, Jonaria," Ferulous greeted her. "But where is Jared?"

"They dragged him away right before you got here. They went down this tunnel," Jonaria explained, motioning to the tunnel. "He can't be too far ahead of us."

Ferulous gave Slag the order to find Jared. The rock dragon perked up, raised his head in the air, and gave three squawks. Then, he took off running down the tunnel Jared had disappeared into. The three warriors followed closely behind him. Eventually, they encountered a four-turn intersection, and Slag stopped. The men holding Jared had split up and taken different tunnels, so Jared's scent was in several tunnels. Slag looked puzzled.

"Did you see this in your vision?" Hurstle asked Ferulous.

"No! We've changed things from what I saw in my vision. So, I'm not sure which direction to go."

"Let's split up into two tunnels," Hurstle suggested. "I'll take Jonaria, and you take Slag." With that, they split up and headed down their designated tunnels. "Are you alright?" Hurstle asked Jonaria as they proceeded down their tunnel. "You're bleeding."

"I'll be fine," Jonaria reassuringly responded. "But Sadean is becoming more unstable. First, he was happy to have me as a captive. Now, he clearly wants me dead."

"Hopefully, he'll keep Jared alive until he gets the ring."

In the other tunnel, Ferulous and Slag were making good time. There weren't many turns in the tunnel, so it was mostly just a straight shot. Slag seemed happy to be with Ferulous. He kept whistling and squawking with delight as they got deeper into the tunnel. And he kept looking back to make sure Ferulous was with him and safe.

Slag suddenly stopped, and his ears went up. "What is it, Slag?" Ferulous asked. Then, Ferulous heard noises coming from ahead of them. It was footsteps, and they were getting louder. After a few moments, Hurstle and Jonaria came barreling into view. The two tunnels had converged. Everyone looked disappointed, knowing they had taken the wrong tunnels. But then, they heard a faint scream that sounded like it was coming from Jared. Hurstle held a light crystal up and discovered that there was a vertical shaft above them. One by one, they ascended the shaft and found themselves in a new tunnel.

Now, Jared's screams were coming from just around a bend in the tunnel. Ferulous pulled out his knife and sword and told Slag to get ready for a fight. They rushed around the bend and straight into the three men dragging Jared away. Slag reared up on his back legs and let out a bloodcurdling squeal. He would not let them continue.

The three men rushed at Ferulous, but they had to get past Slag first. As one of the men was about to swing his sword at Slag, there was another voice that echoed in the tunnel. "Stop! I'll deal with this!" There stood Sadean with his sword in his hand, ready for battle. Sadean's three men parted, letting him walk past them.

The three warriors and Slag stood their ground as Sadean approached. "Let me have the boy, and I'll let you live," Sadean demanded.

"You stay here. I'll handle him this time," Ferulous said to the other two warriors. Swords went up, and Ferulous and Sadean charged each other. A clanging of swords echoed through the dense passageways. Sadean thrust his sword straight at Ferulous, but Ferulous deflected it to the side with his arm, which was shielded with a leather wrap. Sadean spun around and attempted to swing downward, but Ferulous countered that attack and every subsequent attack as well.

Ferulous pulled out a knife, and with the knife in one hand and sword in the other, he was ready to end this skirmish. He knew there was only one way to end it, which was to put a knife into Sadean's heart. As Sadean lifted his sword over his head, Ferulous saw that it was the perfect time to launch a blade at him. He was a master knife thrower.

With one quick motion, Ferulous took the knife blade at the tip, pulled back his arm, and thrust the arm forward with a snap of his wrist. The blade went twirling in the air so fast that it was only a blur. The point of the blade struck Sadean directly in the location of his heart, but the knife simply bounced off and fell to the ground. Sadean laughed as he pulled open his shirt, exposing a thin metal panel that lined his entire chest wall.

"Now, it's my turn!" Sadean yelled with fury. Sadean pulled a knife and flung it at Ferulous. Ferulous was so discombobulated from his failed attempt at Sadean's life that he did not have time to react. The knife struck Ferulous in the chest. But this time, the knife bounced off, too. The knife had been stopped by the ring, which Ferulous was carrying in his front shirt pocket.

Sadean and Ferulous now both stood there in bewilderment. "Now, how did you do *that*?" Sadean demanded to know. Ferulous placed his hand in his front pocket, fished around, and pulled out the ring. Sadean's face went stone cold. "Give me that ring!" he shouted.

"Jared, take this!" Ferulous shouted as he tossed the ring to him. Jared caught the ring and slid it onto his finger until it was snug against the ring from Emera again. The three men holding him let him go and backed away in fear.

The look on Sadean's face was stone-cold. "Give me that ring!" he repeated with even more fury.

"Slag, get Jared out of here!" Ferulous yelled. The rock dragon squawked at Jared to follow him and then led the way to an exit. Ferulous stood his ground so that neither Sadean nor his men could pass him to go running after Jared.

Sadean, knowing that the ring was down there with them, was eager to get the fight over with so he could go after Jared. He lunged at Ferulous, plunging his sword into his chest. The blade missed Ferulous's heart, but it went all the way through him, puncturing muscle, tissue, and lung along the way. Not wanting to waste any more time, Sadean immediately withdrew the blade and went running after Jared.

Hurstle let out a battle cry and barreled toward the three men Sadean had left behind. He hit all three of them at once, knocking them all down under his tremendous force. One by one, they expired to their graves.

Jonaria began tending to Ferulous. She had seen this type of wound before and knew how to treat it. But the longer they waited, the more air pressure would build up in Ferulous's chest cavity and the more his lung would deflate. Jonaria remembered seeing a pool of tar in one of the tunnels they had run through. She figured if they could use it to seal the hole in Ferulous's back, they could then create a flutter valve on his chest to allow air to exit but not return to his chest cavity.

Hurstle and Jonaria helped Ferulous up and started carrying him back the way they had come. Ferulous protested, telling them to leave him and go after Jared. Hurstle and Jonaria knew he was right; they could not leave Jared now. "I'll stay here with Ferulous," Jonaria offered. "You go after Jared." Hurstle nodded in agreement and took off running in the direction he had last seen Jared and Slag headed. For as big as he was, Hurstle was quick and was sure he could catch up to them quickly.

Chapter 19

Tunnel Chase

WHILE HURSTLE WENT to locate Jared and Slag, Jonaria went about trying to find a way to treat Ferulous's chest wound. Jonaria helped Ferulous walk as he lost a lot of blood. She was concerned that they might not make it back to the pool of tar they needed to seal Ferulous's wound and that he might die. "I can't go any further," Ferulous said with a faint voice. He collapsed on the ground. "I can't breathe enough air."

"You must get up!" Jonaria pleaded. "Force yourself to keep moving! Don't quit on me!" She had secretly always loved Ferulous.

At the same moment, Hurstle was barreling down the tunnel where he had last seen Jared as fast as he could, hoping he could get to Jared before Sadean did. He was so focused on saving Jared that he had no idea how far he had run. Suddenly, he found himself back in the green and black crystal chamber. Just being in the chamber was hypnotic, and Hurstle stopped running and found himself staring into an emerald wall. He became so mesmerized by the smoky black waves inside the green that soon, he was no longer thinking about Jared.

As Hurstle stood there looking into the green wall of crystals, he noticed that he was having an out-of-body experience. He could see himself standing there, looking into the green abyss. He could also see the future unfolding before him. He could see Ferulous lying on the rocky ground in a puddle of blood, with Jonaria standing over him, weeping. Ferulous had succumbed to his wound. But that vision disappeared as fast as it had arrived.

Then, Hurstle had another vision. He was watching Jared. Sadean had caught up with Jared, taken the ring back from him, and killed him. Eventually, Hurstle snapped back into his own body, not realizing that he had been standing there for over twenty minutes. Thinking about what he had seen in the green wall, he wept in despair for having lost both his best friend and the boy he had sworn to protect. In his mind, he had failed his mission.

Hurstle remembered what Ferulous had told him about the green wall. Ferulous said that the wall does not necessarily show you what *will* happen, only what *could* happen if you take a certain path. Hurstle was not sure what path would lead to both Ferulous and Jared dying. But he knew he could only continue on one path: the path of trying to save Jared. With all his might, Hurstle called out, "Save Jared!" The words echoed in the green and black chamber. With a light crystal in hand, Hurstle started running through the tunnels again, trying to catch up to Jared before the vision in the green wall became a reality.

Jared and Slag were also running through the tunnels, when suddenly, Jared felt his arm slice open on something sharp. As he yelled out in pain and turned around to see what had cut him, he felt the ring slip off his finger. Sadean stepped out of the shadows, holding a bloody sword and the ring, and said, "Foolish boy! This ring only protects you if you know how to use it. But don't worry; I'll give you a choice. You can either stay here and bleed to death, or I will use the ring to heal you but you must let me use you to get the amulet from the queen."

Jared's arm was bleeding badly. He didn't have long to think but could sense that he would die if he did not allow Sadean to heal him. Feeling lightheaded, he decided he would allow Sadean to capture him once more. He figured that Sadean would try to get the amulet back no matter what, so with Jared being one of the few remaining heirs to the throne, why not try to save his own life in the process? "I'll do it," Jared finally said. "I'll come with you to the palace and convince my mother to turn over the amulet." But Jared hoped things would never get that far.

"Excellent choice," Sadean responded. As Sadean approached Jared, Slag prepared to lunge, but Jared told him to stand down. Sadean tied Jared's hands behind his back and told him to start walking.

"I thought you said you would heal me," Jared protested.

"Let's wait until we're out of the tunnels first," Sadean responded. "I want to make sure none of your warrior friends are hiding out, waiting to pounce on me."

Jared felt he had been had. He nodded to Slag to continue

his attack. Slag lunged forward, ready to sink his teeth into Sadean. But Sadean was now wearing the ring, and as he pressed it against the rock dragon's neck, a shock went through Slag and rendered him unconscious. Sadean returned his attention to Jared and pressed his sword into Jared's back. "You're coming with me now. We're going to get the amulet from your mother." Sadean led Jared to an exit and said, "Keep up with me if you don't want to die in the desert." They began the slow walk to the palace.

Back in the tunnels, Ferulous's chest wound was so excruciatingly painful that he felt like his chest was going to explode. He had lost so much blood that he also felt dizzy and weak. He looked at Jonaria and calmly stated, "I'm dying. This is part of the vision I saw in the green tunnel. I die, and so does Jared. You must leave me here and see if you can change the vision. Hurstle will need your help."

Jonaria welled up with emotion and told Ferulous he can't die because she loves him. Tears rolled down her face and fell onto Ferulous. With all the strength he had left, Ferulous raised his hand to her cheek and brushed his fingers along her face. "I have always loved you, too." Then, his hand fell to his side. His eyes got glossy, and his breathing stopped.

Jonaria watched the life exit Ferulous's body. For a few moments, she stood there in disbelief that he had died. Then, she cradled Ferulous in her arms, with his head on her shoulder. She stayed by his side, crying. But she knew he was right; she must help Hurstle save Jared and the entire Kingdom of Onteria.

Chapter 20

Power Struggle

WITH FERULOUS DEAD, Jonaria was alone in Sadean's tunnels. She knew she needed to track down Hurstle or find an exit or both. Before leaving Ferulous's body behind, Jonaria took his knives and sword. She particularly wanted the knife Ferulous kept strapped to his right side, which was made from metal mined from Olna Mountain and was unbreakable. The knife had been gifted to Ferulous by his father, who had received it from his father. Jonaria knew that Ferulous would want it used in the fight against Sadean, so she took it and began making her way through the tunnels again.

As Jonaria made her way through the tunnels, she heard a group of beasts descend on Ferulous and begin feasting on the once-formidable warrior. She paused and hung her head in despair but then reminded herself out loud, "Keep going." As she began to walk again, she swore she heard a voice tell her to run, but she looked around and didn't see anyone. Then, Jonaria recognized the voice as Ferulous's, telling her in her head that she needed to get moving. She picked up her pace and was

171

soon running through the tunnels as fast as she could.

Jonaria eventually found herself in the green cavern. She, too, was mesmerized by the green crystals with smoky black clouds running through the walls. She found herself standing in front of the main wall, looking at her reflection. It was as if she was being held in that spot by a mysterious force. Within the wall, she saw herself unable to save Ferulous. She started crying, and suddenly, Ferulous's voice returned inside her head and said, "Go save the boy!" But Jonaria remained entranced by the wall, no longer able to tell what was real and what were mere visions from within the wall.

Jonaria felt as though she was running through the cavern of green crystal, but the cavern seemed to never end. She just kept running until, finally, she found an exit to another tunnel. But she blinked hard and suddenly found herself back in front of the green crystal wall, looking into it. She felt stuck there. Then, she heard the voice again: "Go save the boy!" Jonaria now knew she was back in her own body, and she was looking at her hands as they rested on the wall. She did not even re-member putting her hands on the wall, but she shook it off and began running through the green cavern. This time, she found a true exit, and as she left the green cavern, she found herself in a mysterious part of the tunnels.

With the aid of a light crystal she carried and with all ene-my opposition seemingly having fled the tunnels, Jonaria was eventually able to exit the system of tunnels completely. She shielded her eyes as she came into the bright sun of the desert. As her eyes came into focus, she saw that Hurstle and Slag were standing in front of her. "Good to see you, my friend,"

Hurstle greeted Jonaria. "We had hoped you and Ferulous would find this exit like we did. Is he far behind you?"

Jonaria's eyes filled with tears, and a single tear rolled down her cheek. Hurstle immediately sensed that Ferulous was no longer with them. Hurstle lowered his head and said a prayer. He then raised his head again and said, "He is still with us, Jonaria. I can feel him all around us. Don't worry; we will get Sadean for all he has done. And we will properly mourn Ferulous once this is all finished." Hurstle swallowed hard, trying to conceal his emotions, and then he continued. "We need to get to the palace as fast as we can. Sadean has Jared . . . and the ring. He is no doubt after the amulet again."

Since the warriors' pack animals were nowhere to be found, they had no choice but to begin traversing the desert by foot. However, they knew that without help, they would only be able to survive a couple of days at most. Luckily, they encountered a gypsy caravan that they assumed the spirit of Ferulous had sent their way. When Hurstle and Jonaria explained to the gypsies what was going on and that the entire fate of the Kingdom of Onteria was at stake, the gypsies happily agreed to take the warriors to the palace. They knew they could not beat Sadean to the palace, but they would get there as fast as they could.

By nightfall the next day, the caravan pulled up to the palace. Hurstle and Jonaria were immediately concerned when they noticed that there were no guards at the gates. They tried opening the main gate to the palace, but it wouldn't budge. They assumed it was barricaded from the inside. "While I was guarding the queen, she told me of a secret passageway leading

173

between the boathouse and the palace, in case I ever needed to usher her out that way," Hurstle explained. "That's probably our best bet for getting in."

At the boathouse, the warriors located the entrance to the secret passageway, pulled out light crystals to light the way, and entered the passage. The passageway was full of twists and turns but no offshoot tunnels that might lead the warriors in the wrong direction. Instead, it was a straight shot to the palace, and the warriors did not encounter any resistance along the way.

At the end of the secret passageway, a door opened into the dungeon below the palace. Hurstle and Jonaria noticed that all the cells in the dungeon were empty. This was another bad sign. All of Sadean's collaborators had been released! Hurstle and Jonaria knew they would be vastly outnumbered.

Hurstle and Jonaria ascended the dungeon stairs together until they reached the palace's main level. Their entire path to the main level was unguarded. Once they were outside the door that opened to the palace itself, Hurstle paused Jonaria before they went any further. "Do you hear that?" he asked as he cupped his hand around his right ear.

"Yes," Jonaria confirmed. "I hear yelling. It's Sadean's voice. And it's coming from the direction of the library. Let's split up and each enter the library through a different door."

Hurstle nodded his agreement, and the two warriors made their way into the palace. As they got closer to the library, the yelling sounded louder. Now, they could hear not just Sadean but Queen Meriza as well. She was trying to bargain with Sadean to get him to let Jared go so that she could tend to her son's bleeding arm. Sadean had wrapped the arm well enough to keep Jared alive as a bargaining chip for a little while, but Jared had lost a lot of blood, and it was only a matter of time before he would bleed to death.

"Please let him go!" the queen yelled again.

"I will only let him go if you give me that amulet around your neck."

"How do I know you won't kill us both once I give you the amulet?" Queen Meriza had no intention of giving the amulet up, but she wanted to make Sadean think she was considering it.

"You don't!" Sadean spat back. The room was full of Sadean's loyal soldiers, and they had the queen surrounded. The palace guards had been overwhelmed and were now locked in the palace's meat lockers. They had been there long enough that they were beginning to freeze to death.

As Jonaria stood outside the library, she heard a light tapping on the wall to her left, which formed part of the kitchen. She went to investigate the tapping. Once she was in the kitchen, she noticed that no one was around—not even the chefs or the kitchen aids. But the tapping continued. She followed the sound and noticed that it was coming from inside the freezer room, which was locked.

Jonaria slowly opened the freezer while holding the knife she had taken from Ferulous at the ready in case someone rushed her from inside. When she fully opened the door, she gasped. All of the palace's kitchen staff and guards were crowded into the cramped freezer room, huddled together, with a few of them already on the ground passed out. When Jonaria realized what was happening, she told them to get out of the freezer quickly and into the warmth. Those that could move quickly hurried out and went into the dining room, where they lit a fire. Those who could not move were carried to the dining room by the others.

Jonaria located Hurstle and motioned for him to come to the dining room. The two of them explained the circumstances to the palace guards as the guards took turns warming themselves by the fire. Once the guards had warmed up enough, one of them gave the order to surround the library. They were ready for a fight, and so were Hurstle and Jonaria.

Hurstle took a step forward, ready to knock down the library door, but the floor creaked under his enormous weight. The creak was so loud that Sadean heard it from within the library and sent a few of his men out to investigate. Hurstle watched as six men exited the library and surrounded him. "I have a message for your leader, Sadean," Hurstle said. "Take me to him now, or I will kill all of you on the spot." By now, Sadean's men knew Hurstle's reputation and that he could likely kill all six of them easily. So, they wasted no time in escorting him into the library to speak with Sadean.

"Where is your loyal band of misfits?" Sadean asked when he saw Hurstle.

"You killed one of them, and the other one, Jonaria, never made it out of the green crystal tunnel. So, I'm here alone. I'm here seeking revenge."

"But you are defeated. You have no army, you fool! Even you cannot defeat all the men in this room." Sadean paused, considering his next move. "Kill him, men!" he finally ordered.

Five of the six men surrounding Hurstle grabbed him, two on each arm and one grabbing his hair from the back, causing his head to arch upward. The sixth man pulled out a sword made from Olna Mountain metal and held it to Hurstle's throat. The man with the blade turned to Sadean, awaiting final confirmation.

"Stop! Don't kill him!" Jared called out.

"I *will* kill him. And I'll kill you, your sisters, and everyone else the queen cherishes if she does not give me what I want. It's time to hand over the amulet."

At that moment, Jonaria rushed into the room. "I wouldn't do that if I were you. If you don't think Hurstle can easily defeat every man in this room, you can bet he will with me by my side."

Sadean gasped. "But you're supposed to be dead!"

With both Hurstle and Jonaria there, none of Sadean's men wanted to go up against them. The warriors' reputation preceded them. Sadean's men had seen what the warriors had done to their comrades and wanted no part of it. The six men holding Hurstle immediately released him. Hurstle approached the man holding the sword, ready for a fight. But the man relinquished the sword to Hurstle without protest.

Jonaria, holding a sword as well, began moving toward Sadean. Sadean raised the same sword he had used to cut Jared, and as he concentrated on the ring on his finger, the sword began glowing with a green hue. Sadean swung the sword at Jonaria. Jonaria raised her own sword in time to block Sadean's, but Sadean's sword simply sliced through hers, leaving her with half a sword. Jonaria threw the remaining half of her sword at Sadean. He cut his hand on it but was immediately able to heal the cut with the power of the ring.

Sadean grinned broadly, knowing that now that he had harnessed the full potential of the ring, he could take on even great warriors like Hurstle and Jonaria. Feeling confident, he moved toward Jonaria with his glowing sword, ready to strike her down while she had nothing to protect her. But at that moment, the queen called out, "Here! Take this," and tossed her amulet to Jonaria. Jonaria, knowing just what to do, put the amulet around her neck.

Seeing Jonaria put the amulet around her neck made Sadean fearful. He knew that he was no match for a warrior wielding the power of the amulet. So, he grabbed Jared instead. Sadean had kept Jared alive this entire time so that he could use him as a bargaining chip, and he now intended to do just that. Sadean ripped the bandage off Jared's wounded arm, causing Jared to begin bleeding to death again.

"No! Leave him alone!" Queen Meriza yelled.

"Now, guards!" Jonaria called out.

The palace guards, who had been surrounding the library, burst in through all of the library's doors. Sadean's men, who had already accepted defeat when they found themselves face-to-face with two of the fiercest warriors ever to live, now threw down their weapons. "What are you doing, fools? Pick those back up!" Sadean yelled at his men.

With Sadean distracted, Jonaria grabbed one of the discarded swords and pulled Jared away from Sadean. Jonaria focused hard on the blade she held, trying to concentrate the amulet's power on the sword. When the blade began to glow fiery red, Jonaria pushed it into Jared's arm, attempting to cauterize his wound. Jared's wound began to sizzle, and he passed out from the pain. But the wound began to close! After a couple of minutes, the bleeding had completely stopped.

Both the palace guards and Sadean's men, who had now turned on him, descended on him. Sadean admitted to himself that he didn't know enough about the ring to use it to protect him from such an onslaught. "It's over, Sadean, my brother," the queen calmly announced. "Give up the ring, and we will let you live." When Sadean refused, the palace guards held him down, removed the ring by force, and delivered it to their queen.

"Lock him up," Queen Meriza told her guards. "Lock his men up, too, until we can confirm where their loyalties lie." The palace guards took Sadean and his men into custody and dragged them away to the dungeon.

Jared was still unconscious, but the queen walked over to him and slid the ring onto his finger. The healing power of the ring coursed through Jared, and within minutes, the color returned to his face and body. Jared woke completely up, alert and healed. "What happened?" Jared asked his mother.

"I'll tell you later. For now, all you need to know is that you are to keep that ring on at all times. Do you understand?"

Jared looked down at his hand and noticed the ring. He turned his hand side to side so that the ring glistened in the library's candlelight. "Yes. I understand," he confirmed.

Jonaria walked over to the queen, took off the amulet, and handed it back to her. "Thank you, My Queen. You saved my life."

Queen Meriza placed the amulet back around her neck. "No, thank *you* for saving *our* lives."

Chapter 21

Power Restored

NOW THAT SADEAN was locked up, Queen Meriza could not resist the urge to speak with her brother, even if it was for the last time. She made the long, winding descent to the dungeons, where she found Sadean locked up and talking to himself. "Who are you talking to?" the queen asked.

"Our father, Gregor. He says you need me to help you rule the kingdom."

"No, Sadean. There is no one there." The queen hung her head in sadness.

"Our father is here. His essence speaks to me. If you don't let me out to help you rule Onteria, then you are going to fail going up against my army of men."

The queen knew her brother had completely lost his mind. "What men, Sadean? Your remaining followers just threw down their arms and surrendered in the library. There is no one left for you—nothing and no one."

Sadean smiled and remained quiet for a few moments. Then, he went back to talking to himself. The queen shook her head and then departed the dungeon in search of Hurstle and Jonaria.

When the queen located Hurstle and Jonaria, she formally passed along her condolences for the loss of Ferulous. Ferulous had given his life to save Jared's so that Onteria could continue to flourish under its rightful rulers. The queen also told Hurstle and Jonaria that from her visit with Sadean in the dungeon, she was more convinced than ever that he had gone completely mad. "He still thinks he has followers out there who will come save him," she said.

Jared was also mourning the loss of Ferulous. Ferulous had been a good friend and a fiercely loyal companion. Slag came over and settled next to Jared. Jared looked at Slag and knew that Slag had lost his friend and companion, too.

The next day, Jared, his sisters, and Slag waited in the library for Queen Meriza. She had told them to meet her there for a surprise. Eventually, the queen entered the library carrying two small boxes. "How are you all doing?" she asked. "It's been a rough few days."

The queen's children all confirmed that they were doing fine. Jared's arm seemed to be nearly fully healed, thanks to the healing properties of the power ring he was once again wearing. And even though Anna always liked to give him a hard time, she was in good spirits having her brother back and healthy again.

"I'm glad to see you're wearing your ring," the queen said to her son. "As the heir to the throne, you are, after all, the rightful owner of that ring. As for you, my daughters," the queen continued, addressing the twins, "please go ahead and open these." The queen handed each of the twins one of the small boxes.

When the twins opened the boxes, they were thrilled to find necklaces. The queen had the kingdom's master jeweler cut two identical small pieces of her amulet off and make them into necklaces for her daughters. "Go ahead and put them on," she instructed the twins. After the necklaces were in place around their necks, she said, "Wear those necklaces at all times. The more time you spend with them, the more you will learn to harness and use the power of the stones they contain. You are also in line to the throne, and the stones will protect you." Queen Meriza smiled for what seemed to be the first time in ages.

The queen's happiness was short-lived, though. Hurstle came rushing into the library, and before he even spoke, Slag could sense Hurstle's intensity and began bouncing around with anticipation. "We've received word from the outskirts of the city that a large army of powerful men and beasts is headed our way. You must get the children locked in their rooms immediately. I will place guards outside each room to keep them safe."

Though the queen was distraught internally, externally, she tried to project an image of confidence and strength. "Everything will be alright, children," she reassured them. "But please do as Hurstle says and go to your rooms and lock the doors. If you keep the ring and necklaces on you at all times, you will be safe. Never remove them." The queen turned to Hurstle again. "Could it be that Sadean was not crazy when he said he had more men out there? Was he telling the truth?"

"From the scouts' report, yes, these look like Sadean's followers. There's no doubt they're coming here to try to set him free."

"They are not getting into the palace this time, no matter the cost," Queen Meriza asserted. "I know what must be done. Let me go to the dungeon to have a word with my brother in private."

Hurstle was not thrilled about the prospect of leaving the queen alone in such dangerous times. But as the queen was the ruler of Onteria, it was her decision, and Hurstle had no choice but to obey it. "As you wish, Your Majesty," Hurstle agreed. "I will proceed to the armory, where we will get all of the knives, swords, archery equipment, and other reserve battle gear handed out to the palace guards. And I already have men going door to door in the city, alerting residents that they must lock their doors, hide, and shelter in place."

"Very good. Thank you, Hurstle," the queen said. She then took a deep breath and proceeded to the dungeon to meet her brother again. As she went on her way, she could hear the palace guards alerting everyone that hundreds of men with beasts in chains had been spotted on the horizon. It would not be long before they reached the palace gates. The palace guards readied themselves for the battle of their lives.

When Queen Meriza reentered the dungeon, she found Sadean still talking to himself. As she looked upon him with sadness, a single tear rolled down her cheek. She knew that Sadean would never be cured of his madness. She knew that he would never stop coming after the ring and the amulet. And she knew that the only way to protect the palace and the entire

Kingdom of Onteria from Sadean's followers was to leave them with no one to follow. Sadean had killed their father, Gregor—their own flesh and blood. And now, Meriza knew she had no choice but to do the same to Sadean.

Queen Meriza approached Sadean's cell and called him over to her. "My dear brother, your army of men and beasts are descending on the palace. I am here to negotiate the terms of my surrender. Please come closer so we can discuss."

A grin appeared on Sadean's face. "I'm glad you've finally come to your senses."

Sadean wasted no time meeting the queen at the wall of his cell. And the queen wasted no time plunging a dagger made from Olna Mountain metal through the bars of Sadean's cell and deep into his chest. The grin disappeared from Sadean's face, replaced with shock, and he gasped. As the queen began backing away from the wall of bars, Sadean reached through them and grabbed hold of the amulet around the queen's neck, holding her in place.

Sadean pulled the queen back into the bars and thrust his own dagger deep into *her* chest. His last remaining spy among the palace guards had proved useful in smuggling the dagger to him. As Sadean slipped closer to death, his grip on the amulet necklace weakened, and both he and Queen Meriza tumbled backward.

Hurstle, ever the guardian of the queen, had secretly followed her into the dungeon, sensing that she might need help. He emerged from the shadows and ran to the queen's side as she lay bleeding on the cold stone of the dungeon floor. He took one look at the queen's wound and knew that even the amulet could not save her now. Hurstle stood, thrust his sword into Sadean's body several times to ensure he was dead, then turned back to the queen, who was holding out the amulet and a package of envelopes tied with a ribbon and stained with her blood.

"Hurstle, my brave warrior," the queen whispered with a wheeze. "Give the amulet to Jared so that he has both the ring and amulet. And give each of my children these letters. The letters represent my final command about a successor to the throne."

"I will, Your Majesty," Hurstle agreed. "Is there anything else?"

"Yes. Take Sadean's body and put it on display outside the main palace gate so that Sadean's followers know their fight is lost."

"I will, Your Majesty," Hurstle confirmed. After the queen took her final breath, Hurstle shut her eyes and bowed his head for a moment of respectful silence. He then arranged with the palace guards to have Sadean's body wheeled to the palace's front gate in preparation for putting it on display to the approaching army. And he sent a scout to deliver a message to the army that Sadean was dead and there was no need to let fly a single arrow.

Hurstle and Jonaria retrieved Jared and the twins from their rooms and ushered them into the library. The children were beside themselves with the news of their mother's death. It was too soon for them to fully process the bravery she had displayed in her final act of confronting Sadean and ridding Onteria of him. But they were also curious about the envelopes they were holding. They each tore open their own envelope and read the note inside through eyes full of tears.

My dearest children,

If you are reading this, then I am no longer with you. My heart goes out to you as you navigate through life without your parents. But you and your siblings have each other. You are all my progeny and will rule the Kingdom of Onteria together, equally, as one unit. Hurstle and Jonaria will be there for you for as long as you need them. You will have a long and happy life now that the kingdom is free of evil. I know you are sad right now and that you feel alone, but remember, you are never really alone as I will join my mother and her mother in the Incognal.

Love always, your mother, Queen Meriza

Within an hour of Onterian time, a group of representatives from Sadean's army arrived at the palace's main gate, demanding to speak with the queen. Instead of the queen, they were greeted by Jared wearing the ring, Anna wearing the amulet, and Stephany wearing the crown. Hurstle stood behind them, carrying the Incognal. And Jonaria wheeled out a cart that was carrying Sadean's body. With Sadean dead and with the queen's heirs in possession of all the power stones, the army's representatives knew they no longer had any cause to fight for or means to win even if they did. The representatives signed a treaty of surrender and returned to the army, telling the men to disband and return to whatever corners of Onteria they had come from. There would be no battle in Onteria that day . . . and maybe never again.

Chapter 22

A Powerful Future

JARED AND HIS SISTERS held ultimate power and an impenetrable bond. They worked together with Princess Emera to plan their mother's funeral. Despite Queen Meriza's death, the Kingdom of Onteria was more alive than ever as all of the fairies and magical beings that had gone into hiding with Sadean around had now reemerged. Onteria was full of magic and happiness the likes of which had not been seen since Queen Olna and Gregor ruled the land.

The ruling siblings gave their father and Sadean proper burials as well. Regardless of any ill feelings toward Sadean, he was family, too. Sadean could not help it that madness had overtaken him. When the people and beings of Onteria saw the siblings' compassion for Sadean, they knew they were in the hands of wonderful and fair-minded rulers.

The twins took their mother's death particularly hard. Despite them being rulers of an entire kingdom, they were still young and needed a mother figure to help guide them. Jonaria recognized this, and as the only remaining strong female figure in their lives, she reassured them as often as possible that she would always be there for them if they needed anything.

At Queen Meriza's funeral, people and beings came from all over Onteria to pay their respect to the queen and her family and to give their blessings to their new rulers. The funeral had magical light shows and magnificent portraits of the royal family on display for all to see. For those members of the royal family who had already passed on, the portraits were accompanied by a written history of what they had accomplished during life and how they had died. Though Jared's father did not have royal blood, he was honored with a portrait and history as well. The queen and her husband had both died protecting their children and the entire Kingdom of Onteria.

When the funerals were over and the ruling siblings got more accustomed to their new lives, Princess Emera reminded Jared that the Incognal had brought him to her, specifically. "We are destined to marry each other, Jared," she urged. "The Incognal demands it. And it's why I gave you that crystal ring on your finger the first time you visited the palace."

"But I'm only seventeen years old," Jared reminded Emera. "I know this sounds crazy since I'm the ruler of an entire kingdom, but I don't think I'm ready to marry someone yet."

"In Onteria, royal marriages happen at a young age," Emera informed Jared. "Queen Olna and Gregor married each other when they were only sixteen."

Jared knew he needed to embrace his new life in Onteria, but he was more terrified of getting married than ruling a kingdom. At least when he was ruling, he had the power ring to help guide him and keep him safe. But he had no help in navigating a marriage.

After a brief period of silence, Emera finally said, "I have been waiting for you all my life, Jared. I can wait some more—until you are ready."

Jared smiled in return. "My coronation is in one month. At that point, I'll be eighteen years old. If I'm ready to rule the Kingdom of Onteria, then I'm ready to do with you by my side . . . forever. Once I'm king, we should get married."

"That sounds like a splendid plan," the princess agreed.

"You already knew I was going to tell you that, didn't you?"

Princess Emera looked at Jared and smiled. She leaned in, planted a kiss on his cheek, and said, "Yes. I've known I would marry you since the moment we met."

The somber mood hanging over the funerals of Meriza, Dave, and Sadean was soon replaced with days of celebrations surrounding the coronation of Meriza's children and the marriage of King Jared to Princess Emera. Jared and Emera lived peacefully with their son and daughter in the Kingdom of Onteria for hundreds of years. Deep below them, in a palace vault, the Incognal glowed green and bright with satisfaction.

From the Publisher

Thank You from the Publisher

Van Rye Publishing, LLC ("VRP") sincerely thanks you for your interest in and purchase of this book.

VRP hopes you will please consider taking a moment to help other readers like you by leaving a rating or review of this book at your favorite online book retailer. You can do so by visiting the book's product page and locating the button for leaving a rating or review.

Thank you!

Resources from the Publisher

Van Rye Publishing, LLC ("VRP") offers the following resources to readers and to writers.

For *readers* who enjoyed this book or found it useful, please consider receiving updates from VRP about new and discounted books like this one. You can do so by following VRP on

Facebook (at www.facebook.com/vanryepub), Twitter (at www.twitter.com/vanryepub), or Instagram (at www.instagram .com/vanryepub).

For *writers* who enjoyed this book or found it useful, please consider having VRP edit, format, or fully publish your book manuscript. You can find out more and submit your manuscript at VRP's website (at www.vanryepublishing.com).

Thank you again!

About the Author

J OHNNIE WEST grew up in Salt Lake City, Utah, where he joined the Army, later retiring in 2015. During his time in the Army, Johnnie was awarded the Bronze Star and numerous other awards for his role during tours in Iraq and Afghanistan and as an Intelligence Analyst for Sapper Company, a unit of combat-focused engineers. He currently lives in Utah with his wife, whom he married in 1991, and he has four children and seven grandchildren. Johnnie enjoys traveling with his wife, visiting Las Vegas, and going on cruises. He also enjoys writing and published his award-winning sci-fi novel, *Alien Orders*, in 2022.